HELLO CHRISTMAS

KELSIE HOSS

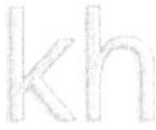

*For my sweet readers who want to enjoy "Happily Ever After"
a little longer.*

CONTENTS

BIRDIE AND COHEN'S CHRISTMAS ADVENTURE

COHEN and I walked away from the Christmas party at my parents' mansion, holding hands. Even though we'd had a good time seeing Anthea and Doug and their two children, and my parents were friendly, there was still heaviness around us as we settled into the car.

Ollie would be spending Christmas with his partner's family this year, which meant we wouldn't get to see him until the new year. I knew Ollie's absence was bringing Cohen's mind back to all of the years when he had to spend special occasions away from his son, sharing him with his ex.

Once we were buckled in, I reached across the console and gripped his hand again. I hated to see him this down, even if he tried putting on a good show for me. "I'm so sorry that we won't get to see Ollie this year," I said, "but I'll try and make it special for you. Okay?"

Some of the sadness left his features as he squeezed my hand back. "Everyday is special with you."

My heart warmed. We had been together over ten years now, and he still treated me with all the love and respect he did when we were dating. He didn't make me feel like a friend or a roommate but someone he truly cherished.

Cold air came from the vents as he put the car in drive and started away from the house. Hopefully the car would warm up soon. It was just cold enough to be uncomfortable. We lived on the opposite side of town from my parents. While their mansion was in a gated neighborhood, our neighborhood had sprawling lawns, tons of color, and all different types of houses.

We had spent hours and days together decorating the house for the holidays, and he hadn't once complained when I wanted to rearrange the Christmas light message on the roof from "Ho Ho Ho" to "Merry Christmas" because it offended our neighbor across the street who could only see one "ho" through their her branches.

I wanted to get him a special present for being so

wonderful, but I was still having trouble figuring out what would be good enough. He had most everything he needed and didn't want for much. So, I planned to stop by the mall later on and do some browsing to see if anything sparked my imagination. Time was running out to get him the perfect gift.

Out the car window, I saw he missed the exit to our house. "You got distracted again," I said. Sometimes he would get so lost in his mind that he would miss our turns and we'd have to go back. A quirk of his, just like I had my quirks, too.

But smiled slightly as he said, "No, I didn't miss our turn."

"Uh huh," I said doubtfully.

"I mean it!" he replied.

I turned and gave him a surprised look. "Where are we going then? It's too cold for ice cream." That was our usual date night go-to. That or the aviary.

Before answering, he reached out and upped the heat. Warm air flowed over me, making my shoulders relax. "Your favorite ice cream shop is closed now," he said. But he smiled a little bigger. "So that's not it."

"What is it then?" I asked, already trying to unravel the mystery.

"If I told you it wouldn't be a surprise, then would it?" He ran his fingers through his wavy salt and pepper hair, far too nonchalant for all the curiosity raging through me.

"It's a surprise right now," I retorted. "I have no idea where you're going."

But he squeezed my hand a little and said, "Let's just enjoy a little Christmas magic." So I sat back in my seat thinking of all the places we could possibly go. There was a light show in the nearby town that we'd been to once and really enjoyed. Maybe he was taking me back one more time before the season was over? There was some kind of puppet market I'd heard about. Apparently every booth sold different types of puppets.

That's when I remembered I had created a spreadsheet with every single Christmas activity within a fifty mile radius so we could make the most of this year. I'd titled it "Birdie and Cohen's Christmas Adventure."

I held up my phone to go through the spreadsheet. Lines with red we'd already done. Green ones were things we wanted to go to. And those in gold were our maybe items. I began looking through the list to see if I could guess based on the direction he was driving.

Glancing at my screen, he said, "It's not on the spreadsheet."

I huffed and crossed my arms over my chest,

making my Christmas sweater jingle. He chuckled at the sound, and I rolled my eyes at him. It was too hard to stay mad at him. So instead, I gave him a smile and searched out the window for hints to our destination. I had grown up here, after all. But the further we drove, I began to realize we were not staying in town.

"Are you going to LA?" I asked.

He dipped his head side to side in a noncommittal answer.

I shoved his arm. "Cohen!"

"Ow," he protested. "No hitting the driver."

I rolled my eyes, remembering that time we were teaching Ollie to drive together. Cohen had flicked him because he forgot to signal. "You sound like Ollie."

"If Ollie doesn't divulge surprises before the time is right, then… yes, yes I do."

"You're no help." I said.

He smiled proudly.

Even though I was acting annoyed, I was actually really touched that he had planned something special for us. I was practically bouncing in the seat by the time he pulled up to the airport. "What's going on here?" I asked. "Are we picking someone up?" My heart raced excitedly. Maybe Henrietta and Tyler were visiting?

He shook his head and held up his phone, swiping the screen to show two boarding passes. I tried to look closer and zoom in to see the city, but he pulled his phone away.

"The flights are for us," he said.

My jaw dropped. "Where are we going?"

"That's for me to know and you to find out later."

"But who's watching Ralphie?" I asked. He wouldn't be okay at home without someone to check on him and keep him company.

"Rory and Beckett are bird sitting," he replied. I also learned that Cohen had somehow sneakily packed bags for us.

There were two suitcases about carry-on sized, so I knew it must not have been a long trip. My mind spun with possible destinations until we made our way through security and reached our gate and I stared up at the sign that said Dallas. "No way," I squealed.

He nodded with a small smile. "I know you've been missing Henrietta."

Completely shocked and more than excited, I shrieked and jumped into his arms, making more than a few people laugh and chuckle around us. "You are the best," I said. "I thought we were just planning on having Christmas at home."

He shook his head. "Home is where you are."

I held his face in my hands and kissed him. "Have I mentioned you're the best?"

He chuckled. "Never hurts to hear… So you're not mad about waiting for the surprise?"

"Not even a little." I squeezed his hand. and then we started my next favorite activity, airport shopping.

I loved going through all of the little stores and seeing what trinkets and books they had inside. Even though I was born and raised in California, I found myself looking at a tumbler that had the state of California with the Santa hat on top. Cohen took it from my hands and said, "I'll get it for you."

I pressed my hands over my heart, and said, "You're spoiling me. I'll go rotten if you keep this up."

But he shook his head and said, "You know rotten fruit turns into wine."

I chuckled at the joke. I certainly did not mind being indulged.

We went to a few more shops, grabbing a book for me to read on the plane and a magazine for him. Soon they were calling our flight to board. We got on board, sitting side by side. Before I even had to worry about it, Cohen flagged down a flight attendant and said, "Can we get a belt extender, please?"

It was easy, with no drama. No guilt or shame. I loved how good he was at taking care of me.

All buckled in, we sat back, talking about Cottonwood Falls and Henrietta and Tyler and the friends we couldn't wait to see. I'd been able to visit Henrietta in Texas a few times over the years, and each trip felt special. She had a really great community around her, and I loved seeing how happy she was to have such great friends and family around. Even if I did miss her more than a little.

I was almost halfway through my book when we landed in Dallas, but I knew we still had a two-hour drive to get to Cottonwood Falls. Cohen led us to the rental car counter, and he surprised me with a rental car that had a Rudolph nose on the front and horns in the windows.

I squealed. "My family always makes fun of me for liking these!"

He shook his head. "I love this about you. Remember, never dull your sparkle."

I nodded in agreement. "I can't wait to pull up to Cottonwood Falls in this."

"Me neither." He said, "Let's go."

2

COHEN

GIVING Birdie presents was the best thing ever, because her whole body lit up with her excitement. She smiled wider, her eyes seemed bluer and she was just so thankful. Her shoulders lifted and she even shimmied with joy. It reminded me of what Ollie used to be like on Christmas morning, tearing through all of his presents.

The memory had my heart constricting slightly. I missed my son extra around the holidays.

This time of year reminded me how I'd only spent half of his life with him because I couldn't make it work with his mom. Even though my life with Birdie was incredible, the shame of my first failed marriage ate at me from time to time. It was hard to think that I'd missed out on so many precious moments with him, but he was a good man, and I knew that he was making memories with family of his own.

The knowledge made me feel more at ease celebrating the holiday with my wife, especially with how excited she was to see her friend.

We took off down the road in the pickup with the gaudiest holiday package the rental company had to offer. She settled into the passenger seat, a Christmas themed throw blanket on her lap, her book open as she read another chapter.

I had my hand on the steering wheel and my free hand on her thigh as I drove to Cottonwood Falls. Dallas traffic was insane and reminded me of LA. Luckily, it thinned the further we got out of the city. When we'd been driving for half an hour or so, I stopped at Starbucks and got Birdie's favorite Christmas drink, a white chocolate mocha, along with a peppermint tea for myself.

Christmas music played on the radio, and between pages she hummed along to a line or two. I knew she felt self-conscious about how much she enjoyed all things Christmas and that her family and even her friends teased her for it sometimes, but her love of the season was one of the things I loved about her. It was amazing how she could boldly go all in on something she loved without letting other people's judgments get in the way.

As we were driving down the interstate, her phone rang and she looked at the screen. With a smile she swiped it open and said, "Hey, Rory, it's so great to hear from you. Thank you for watching Ralphie!" I heard the mumble of a voice on the other end as I turned the volume down. "That was so sweet of you to call. Merry Christmas to you too, sweetie. Tell Beckett I said hello."

I smiled over at my wife. Rory had been one of her students, but over the years she and her husband Beckett had become friends with us. It was fun to see life come full circle that way.

When Birdie had hung up, I asked, "What did Rory have to say?"

"She just wanted to say have fun on my trip and that Ralphie had settled in well at their place." Birdie shook her head. "I can't believe neither of you let the surprise slip!"

I nodded proudly. It was hard to keep secrets, even fun ones like this. "Rory helped me pack the bags for you. I wanted a woman's opinion to make sure you had everything you needed."

"Smart," Birdie replied before taking a sip of her mocha. Then she looked out the window. "Oh my gosh. Ten miles to Cottonwood Falls!" I followed her gaze to the sign.

"I have a little stop for us first," I said.

Her eyebrows scrunched together. "Aren't we going to Hens?"

"Eventually," I teased. Instead of going into town, I turned down a dirt road, following the directions that Liv had given me.

Several miles down the dirt road with dust billowing behind us, we were approaching our destination. And even though it was dark outside, I wanted to be extra cautious not to spoil the surprise. "Birdie, I need you to close your eyes now."

I glanced over at her to find her eyes squeezed shut, a grin on her face. "I can't wait."

3

BIRDIE

COHEN'S HANDS were warm on mine as he helped me out of the car.

I carefully set my foot on what felt like cement. "You're not going to let me trip over anything, are you?" I asked.

He huffed out a grunt. "That was only one time."

"Yeah, and the chicken nearly didn't recover." I said, referencing the time he surprised me with a trip to a farm-to-table themed bed and breakfast.

"She made a full recovery," Cohen reminded me. "No need to feel guilty."

"But I cock-a-doodle-doo." I replied, cracking up at my own jokes.

Cohen sighed, but I could sense him holding

back a smile. "Get thoughts of chickens out of your mind and enjoy this."

"Okay," I huffed, shuffling my feet slowly over the concrete, just in case. At least I didn't hear any chickens nearby.

After passing over gravel and then grass and another sidewalk, we came to a stop and Cohen said, "Are you ready?"

"Yes, I've been ready since you missed our turn." I teased.

He argued, "I didn't miss our turn!"

"I'm not so convinced. You just didn't want to admit it."

He chuckled. "Okay, on the count of three. One, two, three."

I opened my eyes, and my mouth fell open as I took it in. It was Liv's guest cottage. I'd been here before, but this time, the cottage was completely decked for Christmas.

The roof had twinkle lights all over and icicle lights dangled from the gutters. Even the door was decorated to look like a Christmas tree in green and red lights. To top it off, a sign hung on the doorknob that said, *Ho, ho ho.*

I laughed. "You did not do all this for me."

He grinned over at me. "Well, to be fair, I had some help."

I smiled, hugging him again and kissed his cheek, a short layer of stubble grazing my lips. "Thank you, Cohen. I can't wait to see inside."

As he opened the door, he said, "I hope you like it, because we'll be staying here until a couple days after Christmas so you and Hen have plenty of time to visit."

My cheeks were starting to hurt from smiling so much, and I thought it would be impossible for me to get any happier… until we walked inside.

The interior was like something out of Santa's workshop. A nativity scene was in the middle of the table on a layer of cotton. All the curtains were red and green with gold snowflakes hanging from the curtain rods. Even the bedding was Christmas themed. That's when I noticed a giant box with a bow on the bed. "What's this?" I asked, going to it like a kid on Christmas morning.

He was smiling too as he said, "You'll have to open it to find out."

I grinned. He didn't need to ask me twice. I went to the present, tugging on the bow and then lifting the lid. There was tons of material and crafting supplies inside, and a card settled on top with my name on the envelope.

I carefully broke the wax seal and then pulled out the card which said,

You have been invited to an ugly sweater party. Just you and I. Once we're done, we'll watch a Christmas movie by the fire. I love you. -Cohen

My eyes were stinging as I read the letter and looked over at him. I hadn't been able to fit in an ugly sweater party this year because the holidays had been so hectic for my friends. Henrietta was living in Cottonwood Falls, and Mara was busy with a deadline for her next book. But Cohen *knew* me, knew what to give me without me even having to ask.

Salt water fell to my lips as I kissed him again and he tugged me close, breathing me in like he can never get enough of me.

"I love you," I whispered against his lips.

I felt him smile against me. "Shall we get started?" he breathed.

I smiled as I pulled back and nodded. We began by getting out all the supplies and laying them out on the bed. "Looks like a good workbench," I said, taking in all of our options and the space.

He rubbed my shoulder and said, "While you get this organized, I'll make us some hot chocolate."

I grinned. "Sounds great."

Within a few minutes, I had several different sweaters laid out in addition to a station with all the pom-poms, yarn, ornaments and anything else you could dream of to stick on a sweater. Plus plenty of glue. As I was admiring my work, Cohen brought me a mug of cocoa topped with whipped cream and sprinkles. I took it like a child on Christmas morning and drank a few sips before setting it down on one of the nightstands.

A glance out of the window gave me a pretty view of the main house where Henrietta's sister-in-law and her husband lived with their daughters. I pictured them all together, settling in for the night, preparing for Santa to come in the morning, and it made my heart melt.

Christmas was one of the rare times that my parents took off work, and actually made it special for us between all of the holiday gatherings we had to go to for their business. I liked the thought of other children having a special experience too.

Cohen picked up a dark green sweater in his size and said, "What should I do with this one?"

I tilted my head. After a moment of thought, I said, "You could make a snowman with the cotton balls."

"Love it." he said,

"And your snowman needs to be holding a drink because you own a bar."

He chuckled. "What kind of drink would a snowman have?"

I shrugged. "A White Russian? Y'know, because it's cold in Russia?"

"Maybe? I've never been there… What about a peppermint Schnapps?"

"Also a good idea. I'm sure you'll come up with something."

He got to work while I pulled out a sweater with a snowflake pattern on it, deciding to add blue sparkly charms on it. After all, it has kind of become my life's motto not to let anyone dull my sparkle.

While we glued and pinned (and let a swear word slip from time to time), we talked about the last ten years and our goals for the upcoming year. Cohen didn't much believe in New Year's resolutions, but I always liked the idea of a fresh start (and an excuse to buy fresh planners).

We talked about trips we might want to take with Ollie and his partner and on our own as a couple and all the things we were looking forward to in the new year. It made me so proud of this life that we had created together. Step by step, even when it looked like it wouldn't work out for us.

Eventually, Cohen said, "I think mine is done."

I squeezed my eyes shut and said. "Don't show me. Let's try them on and surprise each other like a first look at a wedding."

He chuckled heartily, "Now you're okay with surprises?"

"Well, this last one was kind of fun," I said, reaching out and nudging his shoulder.

With a smile, he said, "I'm down for seeing my bride."

I folded my sweater in half and said, "I'll go to the bathroom. You change out here." Once he agreed, I left the living room. Safely inside the bathroom, I examined the sweater. I'd put so many jewels on the sweater, it had to be at least ten pounds heavier than it was when I started.

Then I pulled off my shirt so I could change. That's when I remembered... I'd worn some sexy Christmas lingerie, planning to surprise Cohen once we got home from the party.

But this would be even better.

I took off my skirt as well and slipped on the bejeweled sweater, wearing only it with a lacy thong and bra underneath.

They matched perfectly.

I couldn't wait to see what Cohen would think.

4

———

COHEN

BIRDIE CALLED from the bathroom like a monster truck rumble announcer, "Are you ready?"

I laughed as I finished tugging on my sweater, making sure that the cotton balls had stayed in place. Like she had suggested, the snowman was holding a drink, but it looked more like a glass of marshmallows than a White Russian.

I said, "Ready!"

I was excited to see her in that sparkly thing she'd made, but my jaw quickly dropped to the floor when I realized that's all she had on.

She looked like a sexy Christmas Eve disco ball without pants on, and then I saw the peek of red lacy fabric underneath to match the sultry look she was giving me.

I scrubbed my hand over my chin, my mouth going dry. "I thought it was supposed to be an ugly sweater party."

She hugged the sweater around her waist and batted her eyes at me. "What do you think?"

My voice came out hoarse. "I think you should take it off."

"The sweater?" she asked, tugging up the fabric so I could see more of her thong.

I shook my head. "The underwear."

Biting her bottom lip, she shimmied her thong down to the floor and kicked it to the side while I began unbuttoning my slacks.

Her eyes drank me in, just as hungry as I was for her. "Are we having sex with our Christmas sweaters on?" she breathed.

I lowered my pants to the floor, showing just how hard my erection was. "Absofuckinlutely."

She giggled, and I said, "Come here."

She walked toward me, her hips swaying sexily.

I didn't even bother hiding how much she amazed me or trying to play it cool. Her body may have changed some since we'd first got together, but I was still enraptured by her.

When she got close enough, I tugged on her sweater to get her even nearer, and some sparkles popped off,

"Oh no." she said. "We're going to ruin it!"

I shook my head at her. "Remember what I said about that dress you wore the first day we met?"

She smiled at me. "It would look better on the floor?"

Instead of responding I leaned in, pressing my lips to hers, savoring the taste of hot chocolate on her tongue, the way her hands carefully and familiarly wound over my shoulders to my neck, tangling in my hair that had gotten a little longer over the last couple months.

Her full chest pressed to mine, and I wound my hand down to her ass, pulling her close.

I sat back on the bed, urging her to sit atop my lap, loving the way her weight grounded me to the mattress.

We teased and played with each other until it was too much for both of us. I shoved my underwear down. She held my gaze as she lowered onto my cock, light reflecting from her shimmery sweater to her face.

I held one of her hips in my hand and cupped her face as she moved over me. "You're so fucking beautiful."

She smiled down at me, swirling her hips in a tantalizing circle, making me moan. "I love you," she breathed.

"I love you so much, Birdie." My voice cracked. Overcome with emotion, I pulled her face to mine, kissing her with every bit of love, every bit of passion she brought out of me.

We made love until both of us were spent, lying half naked in the bed with nothing on but our sweaters. As our breaths started to slow, she propped herself up on her elbows, looking over at me.

"I have a confession," she said, her gaze fidgeting away from mine.

My eyebrows drew together. "Is everything okay?"

Tears filled her eyes as she shook her head. My heart pounded with worry as I sat up. "What's going on?"

Her voice wavered. "I didn't get you a present. And you did all of this for me." She sniffed. "I'm so sorry. Just nothing seemed right."

"Birdie," I breathed, pulling her into me while she cried.

"I'm sorry."

I held her face in my hands so she had to look at me—had to see me.

"Listen to me, babe," I said, brushing the tears from her cheeks. "This life we have together? That is the gift." I meant every word.

MARA AND JONAS VS. THE CHRISTMAS ROMANCE NOVEL

1

———

MARA

I LET OUT A FRUSTRATED GROAN, shut my laptop and folded myself over the desk. My laptop was still warm under my cheek as I lamented this deadline to myself.

Why had I agreed to write a Christmas romance? And *why* had I agreed to get it to my editor on January second?

My publisher was going to be releasing it the following year, but he needed it soon so there was time for editing, cover design, and marketing. Which I understood; I had written and released dozens of books at this point, but somehow this story was coming as more of a challenge than others.

Probably because I had never written a

Christmas romance before. I'd done hockey romance, love at first sight, enemies to lovers, and even a monster romance for fun one Halloween. But something about a fluffy holiday love story did not work with my muse, which annoyed me to no end. I didn't like feeling out of control, especially when an entire publishing house was waiting on me to deliver.

Footsteps sounded behind me, and then Jonas's warm hands found my shoulders, rubbing gently.

"That feels amazing," I said.

"You're pushing yourself too hard," he replied softly.

I sat up to face him, making my office chair squeak. "I have to get this done in eight days, and I still have a quarter of the book left." My heart sped up with my panic.

He took my hand, pulling me to the cushy white chair in the corner of my office. Then he sat down and tugged me onto his lap.

I let myself be held by him as he stroked my arm and said, "Do you remember when you wrote that hockey romance?"

I nodded. That book had practically flown from my fingertips.

Jonas said, "We went to an entire season's worth of NHL games. You were in the locker room, talking to players, interviewing the coaches, schmoozing reporters who interviewed players. You were listening to podcasts all the time. But as far as I can tell, you haven't gotten into it with this book like you have with others."

I wrapped my arms around him and leaned my head on his shoulder. "You're right." He was usually right, even if I didn't like to admit it all the time.

He squeezed me back. "You've had problems with Christmas for as long as we've been together. I feel like you tolerate the season, but you don't enjoy it."

My eyes started to sting with tears, and I nodded. I didn't know how I'd gotten to be in my forties and still was affected this much by my upbringing. I hadn't seen my mom since I was sixteen years old. At least my dad and I had made amends before he passed away the year before. I cherished the relation- ship I'd gotten with him, but now that was over.

"Maybe I just didn't get the Christmas gene," I sniffed.

Jonas tilted his head to the side. "Well, I've had *decades* of Christmases to practice enjoying the season. So what if we do a crash course on Christmas?"

I gave him a skeptical look. "I'm not sure I have

time. You know I have to write ten thousand words by the first, right?"

He shrugged, seeming unconcerned. "So you could stay here and bang your head against the keyboard–literally–or you could come get inspiration with me… Or, you know, you could tell your editor you didn't get it done in time."

"Yeah, because she'll be totally happy with that," I replied.

He chuckled. "You're the talent, darling."

I shook my head, sitting up in his lap. "What did you have in mind?"

Now he was smiling excitedly. "Go put on your ugliest Christmas sweater, that one Birdie gave you a few years back. I'll be waiting in the car."

My editor would kill me if she knew how behind I was and now going on a crazy adventure. But how could I turn down a chance to go on an adventure with the love of my life? "I guess a day couldn't hurt."

He grinned. "A day is all we need."

I gave him a kiss before getting out of his lap and going to the bedroom. I changed out of my pajamas and went to my closet, tugging out the sweater that made me look like a Christmas tree when I put my arms above my head. I had barely managed to wear it for the night that Birdie gave it to me because it was just so ridiculous. But I was also relieved to be spending time with Jonas and getting away from the computer and the story that simply refused to fall into place. So I finished getting dressed and went out to the driveway.

California winters were mild, so Jonas was sitting there with his window rolled down, and *"Here Comes Santa Claus"* was blaring over the speakers.

"You're lucky you're cute," I said over the music.

He waggled his eyebrows. "That's why you agreed to come along, right?"

"Partially?" I teased.

He smiled at me as I went to the passenger side and got in. "So where to first?" I asked.

"We'll start with the age-old holiday tradition," he said, backing out of the driveway. "We're going to the mall."

I gave Jonas a horror-stricken look. "The mall? You know I avoid that place from November to January."

"Exactly," he replied, "but most people don't, so let's check it out."

Jonas drove the twenty minutes or so from our home to the closest mall, and just as I expected, the parking lot was completely packed with people. We finally found a spot that felt like it was a mile away.

As I got out of the car I said to him, "Good thing these Uggs are comfortable."

"All part of the Christmas charm," he replied. "Come on." He laced his fingers through mine, and I leaned my head on his shoulder for a moment. He had on the sweater his mom had knitted for him a couple of years before.

She had taken up audio books, and knitting was the perfect way to busy her hands while she listened to stories, especially because her house was far too full of paperback novels to ever store any more.

"How does it feel to be in the daylight?" he asked me as we wound through cars in the parking lot.

I hissed. "You know I'm a vampire when I'm on a deadline."

"Wrong holiday," he replied.

I chuckled. "Maybe I'm just like those mean reindeer, then. You know they only come out at night."

"Olive," he corrected.

I drew my eyebrows together. "Who's Olive?"

He sang, "Olive the other reindeer."

I rolled my eyes at him, laughing despite myself. The dad jokes were one part ridiculous and one part endearing, and his nieces and nephews loved them.

We hadn't had children of our own, but we also had so much fun keeping Tessa's children for a week at a time over summer break and as many weekends as we could. It was so fun to watch them but also get a break when we were done.

We finally made it into the mall and Jonas led me to a long line.

I froze in place. "Oh, hell no."

Jonas said, "What's a Christmas romance without sitting on a sexy Santa's lap?"

2

___

JONAS

I STOOD next to my wife in the insane line that wound through the atrium. Since it was Christmas Eve, the place was completely packed with tourists and families.

So I held Mara's hand as we stepped into place behind a set of parents and their two small children. One of them was crying while the other one watched Bluey on a cell phone. The parents tried—and failed—to soothe the crying child with hot chocolate.

I leaned closer to Mara and whispered, "Any inspiration striking?"

She looked over at me. "The inspiration to go back home."

I laughed and rubbed her shoulder. "That's the spirit."

We were quiet for a moment, and I watched her focus slip away. She was daydreaming, like she often did. Her head lost in story worlds, couples falling in love, families coming together, friends supporting each other… Everything that made a Mara Taylor romance something special.

I loved watching her eyes flick around the setting, thoughts piecing together that were wholly her own.

The child ahead of us stopped crying, a big ring of hot chocolate on his lips. I chuckled at the sight. "You're doing a great job," I said to the parents.

They gave me a grateful smile, and the dad said, "Trying to."

When I decided to be with Mara, I thought maybe it would be a big deal that I wouldn't be a father, but I found that my life was full now. I was able to be there for my parents without having to put a child first. I got to spend time with my sister and her husband and their growing family. I could travel with my wife as her career grew and expanded and changed. Not to mention, it had given me time to build the business of my dreams, one that treated its workers with dignity and respect and understood that they had lives outside of work. It was the thing that I was most proud of.

Mara and I had made a beautiful life together.

Slowly, the line moved us closer and closer to Santa Claus.

It was a strange tradition, if you thought about it, bringing your children to a man in disguise to have them sit on a total stranger's lap and tell him their wishes.

But there was so much magic in it too, and I could see from Mara's expression that she thought it was cute as well.

Eventually, we got to the front of the line. As Santa looked up at us, I could tell he was exhausted. Despite the tired bags under his eyes, he said, "Ho, Ho, Ho! Is there a baby on the way?"

Mara and I cringed at each other. She confided in me once that it really hurt her feelings when people assumed she was pregnant because of her size, but I was proud of the way she responded. She lifted her chin and said, "A book baby. I'm writing a story about Christmas and wanted to meet Santa."

With his face looking especially flushed, he said, "All right then, sit on Santa's lap."

She took him in and said, "I think I'm good."

I snickered to myself as we walked away. "Rejected."

Mara rolled her eyes at me. "You would think a man who is notorious for having a big belly wouldn't prejudge a woman. I'm *so* glad I made it out of the house today."

"Just another day in Christmas paradise," I said. Then I put on an Olde English accent and added, "But fear not, m'lady; there are better things in the mall than this."

"Like what?" she replied skeptically.

"Like the food. Obviously." I said with a laugh.

For the next hour or so, we walked through the mall finding all of my favorite holiday treats. There were roasted candy nuts, minty Christmas drinks, hot chocolate, peppermint candies, and more. It was fun to meander around with her, commenting on anything and everything.

She looked over at me and said, "Thank you so much for bringing me out of the house. It's been nice to get a break from the computer."

I nodded, "Of course." I noticed she had a crumb from the candied nuts on her cheek, and I said, "Hold on, let me."

We stopped in the walkway, people parting and walking around us as I leaned in and kissed the crumb from the corner of her lips. Sweetness flooded my tastebuds, and warmth flowed through my veins.

She smiled up at me, her eyes warm and bright.

"You know something?" I asked.

She looked up at me, waiting for my answer.

"Even though you don't like Christmas… you embody all that it is." I cupped her cheek with my hand. "Love, family, warmth, creativity… You're amazing, Mara."

"I've never met anyone more warm or loving than you, Jonas," she replied, winding her arms around my waist. "You're the best partner, the best friend, I could have ever dreamed of. Better than anyone I could imagine and put on paper."

My chest lifted at her words, and she reached on her tiptoes to kiss my lips.

We kissed for only a moment before someone behind us shouted, "Get a room!"

She chuckled while slipping her hand in mine and said, "What's next?"

We started walking again with the flow of people, and I said, "This is going to be a treat."

3
———

MARA

JONAS GUIDED me toward one of the department stores and said, "We have to get a last-minute Christmas gift."

I raised my eyebrows. "I mailed out everyone's gift cards weeks ago."

"I know, but this is part of the mall experience," he replied as he picked up a bottle of cologne shaped like a robot. One spray had him wincing and setting it back down.

"I guess I'm along for the ride," I said, picking up a different bottle of cologne and examining the design. "Who should we shop for?"

"We should get something for our neighbor. Mr. Kilgore."

I raised my eyebrows, "But he's so grumpy. Do

you remember the face he made when he found out I'm a romance author?"

"That's exactly the point," Jonas said as he tugged me toward the crowded discount section. "That's why we're shopping when all the good gifts are gone."

I had to laugh. "Okay, let's go see."

We spent the next half hour wandering through the store and wondering what the best bad gift could be. A bread maker? No one made bread anymore when you could get a loaf at the store for a few dollars.

A loud chew toy for his dog? Maybe.

We finally settled on a giant popcorn machine, and I was giggling all the way as we wheeled the thing through the parking lot and back to the car. "Okay, maybe the mall is not so bad at Christmastime." In fact, I'd had such a good time, I only realized we'd been there for four hours when we were back in the car.

"How were we in there so long?" I asked him. "I should probably get back to writing."

But he shook his head. "You said you'd give me a day, not half a day."

Even though I was still nervous about my deadline, I gave in. "I guess you're right. Where to next?"

He put the car in gear and didn't stop driving

until we reached a maker's market happening down-town. Most of the surrounding roads had been blocked off, giving way to hundreds of sellers oper-ating out of white tents.

People selling handmade pottery, food, choco-lates, ceramics–pretty much anything you could stick a price tag on. We held hands as we wandered up and down the rows, sampling, tasting, and buying more than we should have. We even got souvenir mugs shaped like a boot and filled with apple cider. By the time we were done exploring, the sun was already behind the horizon, giving way to muted shades of pink and orange.

I smiled over at Jonas. "Okay, that was a good idea. Have you been to this event before?"

His cheeks gained a bit of color as he admitted, "Birdie sent me her spreadsheet of Christmas activi-ties. It's titled and color-coded and everything."

The look on his face had me letting out a hearty laugh. "Of course she has an entire spreadsheet of Christmas activities in town… Well, what's next on the list?"

"No hustling back home to write?" He gave me an impressed look, and I bumped his shoulder. He chuckled and said, "I saved the best for last. Christmas lights in the park."

I smiled. "That sounds fun."

"There's even an ice skating rink there."

I raised my eyebrows. "You want me to ice skate? We both know SoCal girls and ice do not mix well."

"But you're married to a Canadian now," he countered. "You have to try it. Whether it goes good or bad, you'll have something to write about."

He knew me too well. And the smile on his face told me he knew that he had won. So when we pulled up to a beautiful park near Emerson Trails, I was already bracing myself to fall down a million times.

Jonas walked around to my side of the car and opened the door for me. "Don't worry," he said as he helped me down. "We'll check out the lights first."

I laughed. "Thank you."

He linked his fingers through mine as we walked through the park, taking in all the different art displays made purely of Christmas lights. I could feel the ridges of my mind tracing the patterns and forming words to describe them. Stringing moments and emotions together the way I'd been doing most my life.

Jonas was so good with me, never getting annoyed when I was lost in my own little world. When I came out of my creative trance, he said, "Y'know planner season is coming up."

That got a smile out of me. I loved an excuse for a fresh start and fresh stationary supplies.

"What do you think you'll write next?" he asked. "After this Christmas book."

I tilted my head. "Not a hundred percent sure." But an idea had been teasing at the corners of my mind for a while. "I think I want to write a series about friends who all get their happily-ever-afters with the men of their dreams. Just like I did with you."

He smiled down at me, Christmas lights reflecting in his pretty brown eyes. Then he tangled his hand in my hair at the base of my neck and kissed me long and slow, not paying attention to the people walking around us or the Christmas music playing over the speakers.

That all faded away until all that was left was our own happily ever after.

When we broke apart, he brushed my ear with his nose and whispered, "You're just trying to distract me from ice skating."

I bit my lip. "Looks like my evil plan isn't going to work."

He laughed, "Not a chance."

This was going to be an adventure.

4

JONAS

GROWING up in Canada before my family moved to California, I knew my way around an ice skating rink, but it was clear by the way Mara was hobbling in her ice skates that she did not.

"Stop laughing at me!" she cried, despite smiling herself. Her cheeks hadn't been this red in a long time.

"You look like you'd rather walk on all fours." I said at her bent-over shape.

In protest, she straightened back up, but then waved her arms wildly, her hips dancing forward and backward as she tried to catch her balance.

I shuffled forward on my skates, grabbing her arm and steadying her just in time.

She looked over at me and spoke breathlessly,

"You know? I think I can grasp the idea *without* being on the ice."

I shook my head. "This is part of the experience. No one's good right away."

"You're just saying that," she countered. Mara was good at so many things that it was hard for her to be a beginner sometimes.

"I'm not. You can do this." I stepped slowly beside her and then carefully onto the ice skating rink. We stayed close to the wall and when she watched a kid going by with a little tripod to help him stand up, Mara said, "I want one of those!"

I chuckled, "They don't make them tall enough for you."

She stuck her tongue out at me and then almost lost her balance and clung onto the wall.

"That's what you get." I teased.

She shook her head and whined, "Tell me what to do."

"So the important thing is to keep your knees bent, keep your center of gravity steady. If you lean too far forward or backwards, you'll slip."

"Okay…" She bent her knees a little bit.

"Good job," I encouraged. "Now, you can keep one hand on the wall and one hand on mine, and we'll take it nice and slow."

She nodded, determined. "I'm so not letting these kids outskate me all night."

I chuckled, loving her competitive spirit. "That's my girl."

For the next half hour or so, we made a grand total of two laps around the ice skating rink before Mara said she wanted to try a lap on her own.

I stepped off to the side of the rink and leaned on the railing to watch her. Her expression was set in one of pure determination as she slowly made her way around the ice. She wobbled a time or two, but she didn't go down. When she reached me, her cheeks were flushed and her hair had fallen from the bun atop of her head, forming wisps around her face.

"I think that's it for the night," she huffed, trying to catch her breath.

"I'm so proud of you!" I replied and helped her to a bench. "Really, that was amazing for your first time."

She smiled over at me, her cheeks still flushed with exertion. "Thanks for pushing me out of my comfort zone. I know I don't say it enough, but I'm really lucky to have you. I feel like sometimes I get so lost in story worlds that I miss out on this one."

I leaned my forehead to hers. "Always."

We shucked our skates and returned them to the

rental counter. As we walked back to the car, she said, "I think I have enough material to get going. Thank you so much for today."

But I shook my head and said, "The day's not over yet."

5

———

MARA

DESPITE MY LACK of skill at skating, I couldn't wait to find out what Jonas had planned next. I was starting to enjoy this Christmas thing, especially with him by my side.

We held hands in the car on the way, but when we pulled into the driveway, I was surprised. "We're staying at home?"

"You wouldn't want to do this in public," he replied, voice slightly hoarse.

My stomach flipped with the insinuation.

"Come on." He led me into the house and farther into our living room, lit only by the red and white Christmas tree in the corner.

Jonas let go of my hand and walked to our electric fireplace. As soon as the flames danced amongst artificial logs, he ordered, "Get naked and lay on the rug. I'll be right back."

My mouth fell open as I stared after him walking away.

When he realized I wasn't moving, his voice grew dark. "Now."

I shivered with excitement, finally taking off this ugly Christmas sweater and my leggings. Then I tugged the hair tie from my bun and ran my fingers through my mane so I could look as good as possible laying on our fluffy white rug.

The material was soft under my bare skin, and I lay back, running my fingers over my stomach, my breasts, watching my nipples form peaks.

I was ready for him. For whatever he asked me to do. Because after all this time, I knew at least one thing for certain: Jonas could make me feel good.

I heard his footsteps on the stone floor and turned to see him walking toward me, naked, with a strand of glowing lights in his hands.

"Hands. Above. Your. Head."

There was no arguing with demanding, dominating Jonas. So I did as he asked, every nerve ending in my body on high alert for him.

He knelt behind my head ,and I shifted back, mesmerized by his thick cock and heavy sack, as he secured my hands in the strand of lights. I licked my lips, wanting to taste him, wanting to make him feel good.

"Beg for it," he uttered.

I bit my lip. "Please. Please let me taste your cock."

"Good girl," he hummed, coming to kneel over my neck. He angled his hips so his head bumped against my mouth. I kissed the tip before opening and sucking him in.

I wished I had use of my hands. But I didn't.

So I took him as deep as I could for as long as I could until I coughed and sputtered on his dick like I knew he liked.

He drew out, giving me a chance to breathe. "Fuck, baby. You know how to please me."

"I do," I said before taking him back in my mouth. Sucking and swirling my tongue until I could taste the first beads of semen.

We'd been together long enough I knew he'd want more than my mouth. And just like I expected, he pulled away from me, moving down my body. His fingers grazed over my entrance, and he smiled wickedly.

"That turned you on, didn't it, baby?"

"You always turn me on," I replied, before he angled himself inside me and showed me pleasure until I couldn't tell if the stars I saw were from the strength of the orgasm or Christmas lights.

When we were done, he carefully removed the strand of lights binding my arms and gently kissed both my wrists. And then I lay on his chest, tracing my fingers over the peaks and valleys of his stomach muscles. "This was the perfect day," I said to him, sated in every sense.

He pulled me closer and kissed the top of my head. I felt so safe. So warm.

"It's about to get better," he said.

I rolled my head to the side to look up at him. "How is that even possible?"

He chuckled. "Go to your office and see."

With a small smile on my lips, I stood, pulling the blanket around me and leaving him bare. He propped himself up, all angles and lines there on the rug. I paused for a moment, taking him in.

"Eyes up here," he teased.

"Can you blame me?" I smiled back and then bent to give him a quick kiss on the cheek before padding to my writing cave.

When I went inside, the entire place had been decked out in Christmas everything. There were colorful lights strung around the ceiling, the comfy chair had a red throw blanket with white snowflakes sitting over the top. And then the free surfaces had been covered with cotton "snow" and Christmas figurines.

And right next to my desk was a picture of Jonas in a Santa suit, the jacket open to show his body. I picked it up and stared at it, suddenly unsure of my motivation to write instead of having more spicy time by the fire.

"Like it?" he asked.

I turned to see him leaning against the door frame, now, regretfully, wearing boxers. "I love it," I said. I went to him and gave him a long kiss.

He mumbled against my lips. "Shouldn't you be writing?"

I smiled. "Sure, Santa. And when I get done, it's your turn for a present. Except I won't be sitting on your lap." I leaned closer, humming into his ear, "I'll be on my knees."

"Best Christmas ever."

HENRIETTA AND TYLER AND THE NIGHT BEFORE CHRISTMAS

1

HENRIETTA

THE THREE OF us lay in our bed, wearing matching Christmas pajamas, all snuggled up under the blankets while Tyler's deep voice hummed the words to *A Visit from St. Nicholas*. I glanced over at him and our daughter, Tatiana, curled up in his arms and listening to every word. I know I thought it before, but I loved him more today than ever.

We'd been together over six years now, and life just kept getting better. First, it was the two of us, taking a leap to make the promise of marriage to each other, then growing our business together, and now, we had the most beautiful daughter with dark brown eyes and soft curly hair.

She was the best of us both. Kind and thoughtful like her dad. Loving and determined like me. Discovering more and more of her personality each day was the highlight of my life. I loved watching the person that she was becoming with Tyler as her dad, me as her mom.

Tyler pointed at one of the pages and said, "What do you think the mouse is feeling right now?"

"Essited," she said.

He smiled, his eyes crinkling at the corners. "I think you're right."

She wiggled happily and then reached for the next page. My parents had read me this story every year, and now we were carrying on the traditions that our families had left for us. Traditions were the ties that bound us, no matter how far apart we were or how much time had passed.

Tyler reached the end of the story and closed the book. Tatiana squirmed, rolling from her back to her belly and pressing her face to the pillow before rolling back over. "I don't wanna go to seep," she whined.

"Are you excited to see what Santa left you under the tree?" I asked her.

She nodded excitedly, sitting up between us. "I weally hope he got me dat Barbie."

I smiled, thinking she would be very pleased with the present I wrapped for her a week or so ago. "All you have to do is go to sleep or he won't be able to come and leave your presents."

Tatiana's eyes widened and she flopped back on her bed, snapping her eyes shut so that her whole face was scrunched. She peeked one eye open to say, "You can go."

Tyler and I exchange an amused look. "Are you sure?" he asked, "I can lay in here with you like usual."

"No." She shoved him before laying back down. "I need to go to seep, so I get my Barbie."

"Okay, bunny." He brushed back her curly hair and kissed her forehead. The tender way he treated our daughter made my heart squeeze with love.

I kissed her forehead, too, before leaving the room.

"Wait," Tatiana said once we were in the doorway. "I didn't get to say goodnight to my baby brudder."

I smiled, walking back over to her bed. She got on her knees and crawled over the blankets to me. Taking my belly in both hands, she kissed my bump, leaving a small wet mark on my pajamas. "Good night, baby," she said.

We haven't settled on a name yet, but she was already so in love, just like Tyler and me.

"Goodnight." I said again, and we walked out of the room, leaving the door shut.

We stalled in the hallway a moment, but when

Tatiana didn't call us back in, Tyler and I went to sit on the couch in our living room.

He leaned in close and whispered, "I know you're excited to get started."

I chuckled. I really was. I had been excited for this moment since before I gave birth to her, and now she was finally old enough to truly enjoy and start understanding Christmas morning.

"Let's wait a few minutes so we can make sure she's asleep," I said.

He nodded, reaching out and holding my hand. "So, I've thought of a name for the baby."

I looked over at him, "Really?"

He splayed a large hand over my stomach, and I swore I could feel our baby lean into his touch. "What if we name him after your grandpa?" Tyler asked.

My heart melted as I studied his expression. "That would mean so much to my grandma."

He smiled. "And to you, I know how much you loved him."

I reached out, cupping his face, and kissed him slowly. He always took his time with me, savoring the moment, even though we'd kissed thousands of times before. When we pulled back, he smiled at me and bit his bottom lip. "How did I get so lucky with you?"

"I think we both are lucky." I replied with a soft smile.

He squeezed my hand then got up and walked to our daughter's bedroom to check on her. I watched him peek his head through the door, and when he came back to the living room and said, "Not a creature is stirring, not even our daughter."

I laughed. "She really is excited for Santa to come bring the presents."

"Well, let's get started," Tyler said, "I'll make cocoa while you put the presents under the tree?"

I nodded, feeling as giddy as Tatiana would be tomorrow morning. I could just imagine her stepping out of her bedroom, rubbing sleepy eyes, and seeing the tree alight and surrounded by new presents. It really would feel like magic.

While Tyler went to our kitchen, I traveled back to the bedroom. My feet and ankles were swollen more than in my first pregnancy, but at least this time, I knew what to expect with my changing body. I walked to the closet and pulled out two boxes with presents, stocking stuffers, and the stocking that Tyler's mom had embroidered with Tatiana's name. Balancing the boxes between my arms and hips, I carried them out to the living room.

The overhead lights were dim, but the strand of bulbs around the Christmas tree cast a magical glow over the room. The hues caught Tyler's form as he stood over the stove, making homemade hot cocoa with one of his mom's recipes.

Smiling to myself, I carefully arranged the presents so that they were spread around the bottom of the tree. Then I tucked any number of objects that we would probably regret tomorrow into her stocking, including slime, plenty of candy, and a few noise makers, plus an orange. My grandma always insisted we had an orange in our stockings, and I wanted to continue that tradition with Tatiana.

Once it was all set up, I went to the kitchen. A metal spoon scraped softly over the pan as Tyler stirred our drinks. I bumped his hip with mine before reaching up for the container of flour. The cabinet was barely open before Tyler came behind me, crowding my back with his warmth. He grabbed the flour and set it on the counter.

"Here you go," he said, and dropped a light kiss on my shoulder.

I nudged my backside against him, about ready to abandon this whole operation in lieu of taking him to the bedroom. These pregnancy hormones were no joke. I swear we could do it all day, every day, and it wouldn't be enough. Not that he was complaining. I guess I had to make up for all those years I spent as a virgin.

"Hey now," he hummed. "I thought you were getting the presents ready."

"I am," I said flirtatiously.

He nipped at my ear, putting his hands on my hips. "Keep playing games, and I'll have you bent over right here."

I shuddered. "Why are you holding back?" I bent over further, wanting him to sate this need that flamed up as quickly as the burner on the stove.

Deftly, his hands slipped under my pajama pants and when he reached my sensitive spot, he groaned against my shoulder. "You're already wet. How long have you been waiting for this?"

"Too damn long. I can't get enough of you," I replied, moving my hips for more friction of his hand.

"So impatient." He slipped a finger inside, making me quiver. It wasn't enough.

"More," I begged, my voice getting whiny.

"Whatever you need." He withdrew his finger long enough to slide down my pants, and soon his tip was at my entrance. I clenched.

"Hurry," I begged.

"I like it when you beg for me," he said, a dark, playful edge to his tone.

"Please," I said, looking over my shoulder at him for puppy-dog eyes. He was so damn hot haloed by

Christmas lights. Eyes dark, jaw strong. Hands digging into my hips.

He drove into me, inch by inch, and the relief was so sweet my eyes stung with tears. "Tyler," I cried out softly.

"I've got you, baby." He ran his hands over my hips, my back, leaving a trail of heat everywhere his calloused palms went.

Bracing myself with one arm on the counter, I used my free hand to circle my clit.

"Make yourself feel good," he said. "Use me, my cock. Make yourself come."

This man. He knew exactly what I needed. And he braced himself for me. Letting me ride him, letting me angle the way that felt just right until I was shuddering, falling apart around him, breath coming just as hard and fast as my orgasm.

As I leaned forward against the counter, he pumped into me, riding the waves of my release to his own.

When we both had caught our breath, he wet a washcloth for me, letting me clean myself up while he attended to the hot chocolate. My cheeks were flushed and warm when I tossed the rag in the hamper and turned to face him. "I don't know where that came from. But thank you."

His eyes sparkled from the Christmas lights.

"Obviously, me getting flour for you is incredibly sexy."

I giggled, feeling light and happy. "That reminds me. I better get to work."

I went and got one of Tyler's work boots, and used it with the flour to create a trail of footprints from our faux fireplace to the Christmas tree. The effect was so adorable a puppy couldn't compete.

Once I was done with that, I got a few sugar cookies that Tatiana and I had made with Tyler's sister, Liv, and her children. As I placed each one on a tray, I took a couple of bites to give the full Santa effect. Then I got a glass of milk from the fridge and set it beside the cookies, stepping back to admire my handiwork. "Tyler, come look," I said.

"Perfect timing," he replied, like we didn't just have hot sex in the kitchen.

I could hear the whoosh of the whipped cream can as he added the topping to the hot chocolates. He came into the living room and passed me my cup, taking in the work. "Our daughter is so lucky to have you," he said.

My heart swelled. "I just really wanted to make it a special day for her."

"It will be," he replied, kissing the crown of my head. "Come sit on the couch with me."

I followed him, going to the couch and tucking

my feet underneath me. Sitting down, I studied my hot cocoa. He had even shaved little pieces of chocolate on top. A sip proved it tasted just as good as it looked.

"I have something for you," he said, setting his cup down on the coffee table.

I raised my eyebrows. "Aren't we supposed to be opening presents tomorrow morning?"

He gave me a look. "You know that tomorrow morning is going to be all about Tatiana, and I want to see your reaction to the present I'm giving you without any distractions."

I placed my free hand over my heart. "That's so sweet."

"You know me," he joked. "So hold still, I'll be right back."

"I'm pregnant and just sat down," I replied. "I'm not getting back up until you haul me out of this chair."

Chuckling, he walked away toward our bedroom.

My mind spun around a dozen ideas of gifts he could have gotten me, but I wasn't confident in any of my guesses. So I sat, not so patiently, waiting to see what he would come back with.

I was more than a little surprised when he returned holding a padded mailer with Christmas designs on it. "You got the mail for me? How sweet."

He rolled his eyes at my joke. "Just open it."

"It's no fair that you didn't come dressed as a sexy mailman," I carried on as I pulled at the flap.

Tyler shook his head at me. "That's something Rhett would do, not me."

I laughed. That was exactly something his younger brother would do. Rhett was always up for a laugh. The plastic ripped enough for me to peer inside, but all there was a sheet of paper. I pulled it out, studying the page. It was a property listing… in California.

"This is my parents' neighbor's house," I said. "Why did you get me a picture of it?"

He took the picture from me and set it aside before holding both my hands in his. "I know that we enjoy our life here in Cottonwood Falls. But I also know you miss your family. Especially with your grandma getting older, time with them feels so precious."

I looked around at our home. It was an apartment in the original Hen House. We had renovated it all those years ago when we were newly married and made this place thoroughly *ours*. "But this is home." I said. Even with how much I missed my family, I couldn't imagine leaving Cottonwood Falls.

Tyler leaned forward and pressed a kiss to my cheek. "This is home, but what if we have a second one right next door to your parents? So over the summers, when the kids are on school break, we can go and stay there, and you can have all the time you want to visit with Birdie and Mara without worrying about crashing on someone's couch or booking a hotel room? The kids will have room to play, and maybe one day when they grow up, they'll want to go to college at Brentwood U. They'll have a great place to stay right next to their grandparents. I know it's *our* money, but I have savings for a downpayment, and I think it would be a good investment for us."

"But how?" I asked, completely stunned. "The neighbors have been living there forever."

"One time when we were visiting, I was talking with them over the fence with your dad. He went to check the grill, and when we got a second alone I said that if they ever considered selling to please let me know. Turns out they're looking to downsize."

My eyes were stinging with moisture, and not just because of the pregnancy hormones. Because he was right, and I was finally letting myself dream about what this would mean.

I missed my family like crazy, and a week or two here and there wasn't enough. I wanted more time to spend with my nieces and nephews. I wanted my children to know their cousins, their parents, their grandparents, their great-grandma.

"I hope those are good tears." Tyler said cautiously as he used the pads of his thumbs to wipe my eyes.

I let out a tearful chuckle. "The best tears," I replied, pulling him close and hugging him tightly. "Now the wallet I got you feels really lame."

He laughed. "This life we have with each other, our love, that's all I need. I couldn't ask for anything more than what you've given me."

Now the tears were full on coming, and since I was so overcome with emotion for words, I poured it all out in my kiss. This was the best Christmas Eve ever, and I knew tomorrow would be even better.

2

———

TYLER

A SQUEAL PEELED through the house. I rolled to the side, taking in my wife sleeping next to me. She had on a black satin bonnet and her mouth was halfway open.

She blinked her eyes groggily and mumbled, "Sounds like Tatiana is awake."

I smiled at her sleepy face, her features more familiar than my own at this point. "I think she saw your Christmas setup."

Her eyes flew open, and she sprung out of the bed faster than I even knew she could with the equivalent of a watermelon strapped to her belly. Her feet tapped lightly over the floor as she went to the living room to see her daughter.

I cast my blankets aside and followed them, just

in time to see Tatiana dancing on the rug, unable to even stand still as she took it all in. Her messy curls waved as she turned and looked at Hen and me, saying, "Santa came!"

Henrietta grinned at our daughter, "How do you know?"

Tatiana pointed excitedly at the footprints made of flour, and then held up a cookie, saying, "Santa ate this! Santa!"

I chuckled at her excitement.

"Can I have the rest?" Tatiana asked.

Henrietta and I exchanged a look. We usually didn't' allow sweets so early, but she was going to have a sugar buzz as soon as we got to Griffen Farms, so I shrugged.

Henrietta brushed back T's hair and said, "Go ahead, baby."

Grinning, Tatiana shoved the whole thing in her mouth, leaving crumbs and frosting falling down her chin.

"Oh my," Hen said, looking horrified.

I chuckled as I shook my head. "She doesn't do anything halfway, does she?"

"Not at all," Hen agreed.

Tatianna picked up one of the presents, shaking it wildly. "Can I open it? Please, please, please?"

I looked at Hen to make sure. We hadn't exactly

discussed a timeline for opening presents. But she nodded, so I said, "Go ahead, hon."

Hen rubbed her back, saying, "We'll sit on the couch and watch you."

While she sat down, I stood behind her, rubbing her shoulders while Tati tore through the first present. Then she tugged my hand, guiding me around the couch to sit by her. As soon as I sat down, she tugged my arm over her shoulders, and I smiled over at her.

Her dark eyes shone with happiness.

I could feel it too.

It was hard to believe that all those years ago, we had been newly in love, making decisions about how our relationship would affect our careers, our families. Now I had everything that had been too outlandish to hope for back then.

A beautiful wife who was the best mother to our child.

A daughter just as incredible as her mom.

A son on the way.

A home.

A life that was better than I could have ever imagined.

FARRAH & GAGE'S STROLL DOWN MEMORY LANE

1

GAGE

I HAD SPENT most of my life being the responsible one, the driven one, because if my life was good or bad, I wanted it to be on me. It's who I am, and I liked being able to take care of myself and the people who mattered most to me. It was rare that someone surprised me.

Someone other than my wife.

We pulled up to Barry and Jenna's place to drop off the kids. They were Christmas shopping with their grandparents while Farrah and I went on a date.

But when the kids got out of the car and inside their grandparents' place, Farrah said, "I have a surprise for you."

I looked over at her, intrigued. "A surprise?"

"And you'll never guess it," she said with a smile. "So I need you to get out and let me drive."

I raised my eyebrows at her from the driver's seat of the minivan. "You want to drive, Miss Passenger Princess?"

She chuckled heartily, "Don't get used to it. This is a one-time thing."

"I wouldn't expect anything less," I teased before getting out of the car. Farrah and I walked around the front, meeting in the middle. But before she could walk past me, I caught her hand, stalling her long enough so we could kiss.

Spending so long as a bachelor, it never escaped me how lucky I was to have this life with her.

Her hands linked behind my neck, and I deepened the kiss, thoroughly enjoying my wife.

But then the front door of Barry and Jenna's house opened, and our youngest, Tara, said, "Ew. Why do you guys always have to kiss in front of us all the time?"

I smiled against my wife's mouth before turning to my daughter. "Maybe because I love your mom, and I hope that one day you'll be with someone who loves you just as much."

Farrah wrapped her arms around my waist and held on tightly. "Exactly."

Jenna came to stand behind Tara. "Couldn't even

wait 'til you got to the movie theater to start making out?" she teased.

Now Farrah's cheeks flushed. "Mom."

I grinned and lifted my hand in a wave. "See you later!"

Farrah and I gave each other one last kiss before trading seats. Once I was buckled in and she was out of the driveway, I asked, "So where are we going?"

She gave me a scolding look, "It's a surprise, silly. Do you want to stop for a little snacky on the way?"

"A snacky," I replied, teasingly. "Of course."

She swung through our most frequented drive-thru and got her favorite snack, fried pickles. We shared the batch as we drove down the road.

"You know what's fun about this age?" she said.

I looked over at her, curious. I could tell she'd been thinking before she brought it up to me.

"They're finally getting to the point where the presents they buy for us aren't just secretly presents for them," she explained.

I had to laugh at that. "You know you could buy anything you want. You don't have to place all that trust in a ten-year-old."

"Sure, and I could also drive every time we go on a trip and get my water at bedtime," she retorted.

"Touché," I replied, laughing. "I have to say, the surprise thing is a little fun," I said.

"Right," she replied doubtfully. "I know the suspense is eating you alive."

"Caught me," I admitted, shifting in the seat. I'd been trying to guess with each turn she made. "So we're heading toward downtown?"

She shook her head at me and let out an exasperated laugh. "Can you just sit back and enjoy the moment?... Never-mind. I know who I'm speaking to."

I grinned. I loved it when she ribbed me from time to time. "You know, you always say that the passenger gets to be the DJ…"

"No," she complained. "Please don't play NPR."

"I like to stay informed," I replied.

"I don't. It stresses me out."

I shook my head at her. We were two very different people, but somehow it worked. She was exactly what I needed when we first met and now, all these years later.

She pointed out the window at the sky-rise where I used to live, and said, "Wave at your old bachelor pad."

I chuckled, following her instructions.

"Do you miss it?" she asked.

"No," I said, "I was never there enough for it to ever really feel like home. And now? Home is where you are."

She smiled, reaching out to hold my hand. I caught her hand, holding it with both of mine. Her wedding ring shimmered on her finger.

"Can I admit something?" she asked.

"Of course," I said.

She bit her bottom lip and then said, "I honestly expected that you would push for a more expensive home after a few years together."

I shrugged. "I know how happy our place makes you, so it never really felt too small to me. It kind of felt like my home growing up."

She squeezed my hand. "You know, maybe now that the kids are moving out and getting older, we could go for something with a little more glitz and glam. They're not so destructive anymore."

I raised my eyebrows at her, "Who are you and what have you done with my wife?"

She chuckled, "You know, we could get a pool, or at least live in a neighborhood with a pool. That would be nice, not having to go to the public pool anymore."

"I'll buy one tomorrow," I said, totally serious.

"Tomorrow?" Her eyes were wide.

"I mean, what did you think was going to happen?" I said. "I want to give you everything, Farrah. Everything you want."

She tilted her head thoughtfully as she drove,

making her curls fall over her shoulder. "I want to home shop. Like actually go to a house and walk through it and see how it feels and imagine it could be ours one day."

"Okay," I said, already getting out my phone to text a realtor friend. "We'll do it."

She smiled. "Yay."

"Does that mean you'll tell me where we're going?" I asked.

She laughed. "Not too much longer."

2

FARRAH

I PUT the van in park and watched my husband's expressions as he took in our destination. He was just as handsome as ever, even if he had a few more lines at the corners of his eyes and his jaw, and his hair was more gray than blonde now. As with most men, he only got better with age, looking more dignified but also more friendly, somehow softened by time and the years we spent together.

There was a soft smile on his lips as he looked from the building back to me. "What are we doing here?"

Even though The Retreat is where we both worked when we fell in love, we hadn't been here in years. Griffen Industries no longer owned it—the business had been acquired by a major hotel group several years prior.

But I said, "The hotel group reached out and asked if I would be interested in a redesign of The Retreat. They liked the original so much but said it's becoming a little dated and it's time for a refresh."

Gage's jaw lowered like he was genuinely surprised. "Farrah, that's amazing. Congratulations. Are you going to take the job?"

"I can't not, right?" I said with a nostalgic smile.

Interior design was my first love, and I'd continued picking up projects throughout the years, even though being with Gage, I never really had a need to work for money. After leaving my ex, I promised myself that I would never be helpless again. I wanted to have a career, something I could fall back on in case anything happened. Something that was just mine.

Gage took a breath and said, "That's exciting, but it feels like the end of an era."

Unclipping my belt, I replied, "I thought we should stay in the Presidential Suite one time before the redesign happens. For old time's sake."

He grinned and lifted my hand to his lips. "I love the way you think."

"My parents agreed to watch the kids overnight, so it's just the two of us. Happy early Christmas."

His smile made the corners of his eyes crinkle more deeply, and then he reached out, pulling me in close for a kiss.

"I love you," he said, and I felt every single word deep in my chest.

"I love you too," I replied.

We got out of the car, and I showed Gage the duffel bag that I had stowed in the hidden compartment of the van's trunk. It was rare for me to pull a surprise over on him, and I was more than a little pleased with myself.

"It was very hard to get the Presidential Suite," I admitted to him. "It's been booked out for months."

"A testament to the great design," he said with a wink.

I thanked him, but deep down, I knew the success of The Retreat was so much bigger than me. Gage had purchased it in an up and coming part of Dallas, and the community had grown around it over time. The travel networks listed it as one of the best places to stay in town, and it attracted everyone from celebrities to the wealthy.

We went inside, and the person at the front desk didn't even recognize us. I wondered what that must be like for Gage, who had been in the spotlight for so long as Texas's first self-made billionaire. But he simply smiled and said, "Reservation for the Griffens."

My heart warmed. Something about all the big and little ways he claimed me as his was still so special to me.

"I've got it right here," the clerk said.

We filled out the necessary paperwork, and soon Gage and I were on the elevator up.

I remembered us in our thirties riding this very elevator, feeling so worn down by our attraction to each other but afraid to give in, afraid to commit, afraid of what would happen if it didn't work out. But today?

Now, I wished I could go back in time and tell myself how far I'd come since a devastating divorce, how far Gage and I had come together.

But I couldn't time travel, so I settled on reveling in the moment as we rode the elevator up to the seventh floor.

But when we tapped the key card to the door and went inside, it was like walking into a time machine after all.

3

———

GAGE

I STARED AT THE SUITE, the prints hanging on the walls, remembering the day we had done the photo shoot together. That had been a real turning point for us, taking our relationship from an agreement to meet our needs to something more.

But I also remembered the day when I first approved the room, when I walked in to see Farrah in the bathtub pleasing herself, my name on her lips.

I was instantly aroused, just thinking of it.

I set the bag down on the bed, and Farrah intertwined her fingers with mine. "I think we should take a bath," she said.

I grinned. "You're full of good ideas today, Mrs. Griffen."

She bit her bottom lip and kicked out of her Ugg

boots. Then she began shimmying out of her leggings.

I watched, rapt. This woman had carried children I loved. She'd held me on my darkest days and celebrated me on my best. She pleasured me in ways I never knew I could be and was a true partner in my life like I'd never experienced.

And damn, did I adore every version of her throughout the years.

I stared as she lifted her sweater over her head and then reached behind herself to unclip her bra, watching me all the while.

My mouth was so dry, I swiped my tongue over my lips. "Fuck me."

Her eyes danced playfully. "I intend to." She crossed around the bed to me, slowly undoing the buttons of my shirt while I ran my hands over her waist, her hips, and back up again. She was so soft under my fingertips.

When she reached the last button of my shirt, she tugged it off my shoulders, pulling it down to the floor, and she knelt down in front of me, now working on my belt.

I dropped my head back, already hard at the thought of what was coming. And then her plump lips were on me, taking in my length. "Farrah," I moaned.

She hummed against my cock, and I looked down at my beautiful girl. I ran my fingers through her tangle of curls. "You know how to make me feel good."

She wrapped her hands around my thighs, using them for leverage until I could feel my tip bumping against the back of her throat.

I brushed her hair back away from her face, tears starting to sting down her eyes until she pulled back to catch her breath.

"You look so pretty when you're choking on my cock," I told her.

She smiled before working back over my length until I'd had as much as I could take. "Let's go to the bathroom," I told her.

She pouted a little, which was almost as hot as what she'd been doing. Then I helped her up, kicking out of my pants and leading her to the bathroom.

It was just as I remembered it–large marble tub, expensive fixtures. My mind's eye saw her breaking above the water, liquid sliding down her full chest as she called my name. Only the sound of water falling from the spigot had me back in the moment, watching Farrah sitting on the side of the tub like a woman in a painting.

Sometimes I wished I had the artistic ability to capture moments like these, when she looked so beautiful it made my chest tighten, my brain straining to remember every little detail.

But then she smiled at me and said, "The water's warm."

I got into the tub first and sat back, my cock still at attention, begging for her. "Sit on me," I ordered.

She lowered herself onto me, each inch I got deeper feeling better than the last.

And then she settled that lush ass on me, burying my cock to the hilt, and moved her hips in a slow, tantalizing circle. "*Fuck*," I hissed.

Farrah was giving me everything, more than I could ask for, and I wanted to make her feel good, too. So I wrapped my arms around her, teasing her clit while the water filled around us. The splashing liquid blended with her moans. And her head dropped back on my shoulder, eyes closed in ecstasy.

"Tell me what you were imagining that day," I said in her ear. "Tell me what you wanted me to do to you."

"I… can't," she gasped out.

"And why is that?" I replied, continuing to tease her clit with one hand, tweaking her nipples with the other.

"Because this feels better," she said breathlessly. "Better than anything I could imagine before I knew how good it was to have your hands on me. Your cock in me."

Her hips were writhing, her hole tightening, and I could tell she was close.

"If it feels so damn good, prove it. Come on my cock. Milk me for everything I have," I demanded before biting her ear, continuing my assault while my cock begged for release.

Her moans came out in pieces until each part of her body tensed, tightened, with her release. It was the permission I needed to let go. To enjoy. To give her every bit of me I had until we were spent, chests heaving as we lay in the tub with water rising around us.

After a moment, she lifted off me and turned off the water, then she lay on my chest and kissed me.

I held her, running my hand over her dark, damp hair as I savored her lips. And then she whispered, "Gage?"

"Yeah?" I asked, eyes drifting open.

Her cheeks were pink, mascara stained around her eyes. "I can't help but think…"

"What?"

"I'm soaking in your cum."

I barked out a laugh—that was the last thing I'd expected to hear. "Shower?" I asked.

She grinned. "Absolutely."

4

FARRAH

MY HAIR WAS STILL DAMP from the bath and subsequent shower as we hung out in the bed in our matching robes, eating decadent treats delivered by room service. I swallowed a bite of my flourless chocolate cake as I looked up at one of the pictures on the wall.

You couldn't tell if you didn't know, but it was Gage and I laying next to each other in bed in robes, holding newspapers in front of our faces.

Even being present for the photoshoot, it was hard to believe it was Gage and me from all those years ago. We were different now—more mature, more patient, more familiar.

Following my gaze, Gage said, "Can we bring that home when you do the redesign?"

I grinned and nodded. "But I think we should take another picture like it. Can you pass me my phone?"

He reached for my purse sitting on the nightstand and gave me my phone, and then I swiped to the camera, holding it out so I could take a selfie of the two of us in our robes, sitting on the bed. Not posed, just enjoying our life together. And I froze the moment forever with a touch of my finger.

We both looked at it for a moment, studying it quietly. I grew misty-eyed before I reached over and kissed him again.

Our relationship wasn't perfectly posed photo shoots. It was us raising children and fighting for what we wanted out of life. It was stolen smiles at the dinner table and the way he always fell asleep holding my hand.

It was *everything*.

LIV AND FLETCHER'S
CHRISTMAS SURPRISE

1

———

LIV

FLETCHER DRAGGED the last of my four Christmas decoration totes into the living room, setting the red and green boxes next to his singular cardboard box. In his chicken scratch doctor handwriting, I could just make out XMAS in faded black Sharpie.

As he stood up and brushed the dust off his hands, he said, "How does one accumulate so much stuff you only use once a year?"

I adjusted my red headband decorated with enamel Christmas trees. "How does one have a child and only have one measly box?"

He shrugged. "My house in Dallas had permanent lights outside, and we did a real tree inside every year... But I'm guessing that's about to change?"

I nodded, going to give him a side hug. My ugly Christmas sweater jingled as I did.

His muscular arm wrapped around me snugly. "I can't wait to see the look on Maya's face when she gets home."

This was our first Christmas as a family. Since she was staying the weekend after Thanksgiving at her mom's place, I thought it would be the perfect time for us to get everything set up to surprise her when she returned.

"Where should we start?" Fletcher asked, game for anything that would make me smile.

I went to the line of my storage totes, reading the notes I wrote on masking tape on the outside. "Let's set up the Christmas tree first."

We pulled open the lid, taking out the flocked tree I'd gotten years ago from Grandpa Griffen. He had no need for it when he downsized and moved into the retirement home, so I gladly took it off his hands.

I had so many memories with that tree. Baking salt dough ornaments with Grandma and painting them with Grandpa before hanging them on the branches just so. Stringing a needle and thread through popcorn and cranberries to make a pretty red and white garland. And then eating the garland and having to do it all over again. Not to mention, the simmer pot Grandma always had going that made their home smell like cinnamon apples and anise.

That made me think… "You figure out this puzzle," I told Fletcher. "It will be like a low-stakes operation."

He chuckled. "You're giving up already?"

I shoved his shoulder playfully. "I'm going to get a simmer pot going."

"Okay…" I could already tell his mind was working to organize all the pieces. This tree was older and wasn't as simple to set up.

I left the living room, walking to the kitchen island with the stove in the center. From here I could see him kneeling on the rug, the pieces spread around him in piles.

I had to smile to myself. If only there was a way to go back and tell my lovestruck, teenage self that someday Fletcher and I would be together–be engaged. She would do a happy dance so intense her hair would get stuck in her pink braces.

Smiling to myself, I set a pan on the stove then got out a cutting board and a few apples from the fruit basket. It took just a few minutes to chop them up and throw them in a pot with some cinnamon sticks and a few pieces of star anise. The sight made me smile. I snapped a pic and sent it to Grandpa Griffen.

Liv: Thinking of holidays with you and Gran. Love you.

Then I set my phone down and returned to Fletcher. He had the base of the tree together, and when I sat next to him, he said, "Hand me a piece from that row, babe?"

"Sure thing." I passed him a branch, and we worked in tandem until the tree was standing—albeit a little crookedly.

Fletcher's dark eyebrows drew together as he tried to adjust the base, but I giggled. "It won't do any good."

"Huh?" he said, frowning over at me. "Is it broken?"

"No, that's part of the charm."

He let out a sigh and then got up and stepped back to admire his work. "I guess we can have a wonky Christmas tree."

I hugged him, saying, "This was my grandma and grandpa's tree. It feels good to carry on the tradition."

He kissed the top of my head. "Then we will—for many years to come."

I smiled up at him, admiring his kind eyes, the angles of his cheeks and chin, his nose. His eyes were so dark, I could see a faint outline of the white tree in them.

"Now we rest?" he asked.

I chuckled, going to the next box. "Now we set up all the trinkets."

I lifted the lid to show all the trinkets I'd inherited or purchased myself since moving out of Mom and Dad's place. There was everything from a white ceramic nativity scene my grandparents had found years ago at a garage sale to the bottle brush Christmas trees I'd snagged at the Target dollar spot.

"I figure these can go on our surfaces," I suggested.

"But where will you put all your new crafts?" he teased. I'd gone through every hobby from candle-making to sourdough bread through the years.

I rolled my eyes at him and said, "I suppose we'll have to be creative. Not that you would know much about that."

He chuckled. "I know, I'm an L-7 square. Just ask my daughter."

"It's the curse of having a daughter—especially a cool one like Maya." Smiling at the thought of her, I said, "Let's get to work."

He nodded. "I'll follow your lead..." Then he paused. "What's that smell? It's amazing."

I sniffed and realized the simmer pot had started to scent the air. "That's the simmer pot! I'm boiling apples, cinnamon, and star anise like Grandma and Grandpa Griffen used to do."

He smiled. "I love it."

"I'm glad," I replied. Then we got to work organizing my ever-growing Christmas decoration collection. Soon every free surface was covered with fluffed cotton batting and little bits and bobs that made the space so much more warm.

"And in the other box?" he asked.

I grinned. "The lights."

2

FLETCHER

LIV'S LIGHTS didn't just go around the tree. Instead, they went on the backs of chairs, on doors, and even around the corners of the room. It was starting to get dark outside when we had set them all up and it was time to turn them on. Half of me was expecting an electrical fire with all these cords around, but Liv was far too happy for me to rain on her parade.

She flitted about the room, checking battery packs, making sure everything was plugged in. And one by one, the strands flared to life, glittering and twinkling about the house.

"Wow..." I breathed, taking it all in. Once again, Liv had turned this place into something special—something magical.

"Wait a second," she said. Then she went to the light switches by the front door, flicking them all off so the twinkle lights were the only source illuminating the room.

"Wow..." I breathed, taking her in. Seeing the lights reflected on her face, battling with her smile to be the brightest thing in the room.

"I know, isn't it special?" she asked.

I went to her, brushing a stray piece of hair behind her ear. "You are, Liv," I said. "I don't know how you always manage to show me that life can get ever better."

Her smile softened, and she stepped closer, lacing her fingers behind my neck. "So the decorations are growing on you?"

I chuckled, running my hands down her waist. "I suppose you could say that."

Her gaze flicked from my eyes to my lips, and soon she was kissing me. Intoxicating me. Enveloping all of my senses.

Her touch was everything and more.

"Come here," I breathed. I linked my fingers with hers, guiding her back to the kitchen island. From there, you could see all the living room and get the strongest scent of her simmer pot.

It was a sight to behold—the trinkets, the light, the

tree lit up and waiting for Maya to put her favorite ornaments on the branches.

"I want you to see all of this... while you see what you do to me."I helped her out of her pants and guided her onto the island, hard marble meeting her soft flesh.

Her smile mixed with her heated gaze sent blood rushing to my cock. It strained against my pants, but this moment wasn't about me—it was all for her.

I helped her out of her top until she was naked save for her red headband. Then I kissed my way down her soft shoulders, her tits, her stomach. I lowered myself between her thighs, multicolored lights dancing over the pale skin.

"Fletch," she breathed, raking her fingers through my hair as I started making her feel good. Licking, sucking, blowing, and adding fingers until she was writhing on the countertop, her walls crushing around my fingers, her voice crying out.

When her orgasm faded, I had just enough time to wipe my face on my shirt before she was tugging it over my head, begging me to get closer to her, to fill her in a way my fingers could not.

I wanted her just as much, relished in her touch, the way her fingers clung to my shoulders, how she reached down with eager hands to guide my cock inside her. The warmth of her pussy, already slick and pliant with desire.

"God, you feel good," I moaned against her ear.

Her breath came in bursts as she rolled her hips on the countertop to create the friction we both desperately needed.

"Lay back," I told her.

And she knew to follow my commands, trusted me to make her feel good.

Her legs wrapped around my hips as she followed my directions–brown hair splaying over white marble, breasts full and heavy.

I pumped into her, pleased to see her body ripple with the movement. She used to be insecure about her curves, but damn she turned me on more than she'd ever know.

I built up a rhythm, driving into her and then drawing back while I tweaked her nipples, rubbed her clit, and dug my fingers into her full hips.

Her noises, her sounds, the way she clenched around me—it was overwhelming. It took all I had to wait until I could feel the start of her orgasm. Hear her gasp out, "I'm coming! Fletcher, I'm coming!"

Her words were gasoline to my fire, drawing every drop out of me until I was spent. Sated. Flushed with her warmth, bathed in her glow.

I took her in, seeing the faint smile on her lips.

"Good?" I asked her.

"Amazing," she replied. She bit down on her bottom lip. "New Christmas tradition?"

I helped her sit up, taking her in my arms and holding her. "From now until forever."

3
———
LIV

FLETCHER HAD GONE to pick up Maya while I stayed home baking Christmas cookies, making popcorn, and preparing needles and thread for us to make a popcorn garland. Maya may not have been my biological daughter, but she was mine. And I couldn't wait to share the holiday with her.

Even if it meant keeping the activities more PG. Just looking at the island made me flush with heat.

I fanned my face before continuing to mix the sugar cookies with red and green sprinkles and M&Ms. The smell of the dough with the simmer pot was heavenly.

I checked my phone for the time—Fletcher and Maya should be home any moment now. But I also saw a new text message.

Grandpa Griffen: Love you too, kid. Thanks for helping me remember all the good times.

I smiled at the text and made a mental note to bring some of the sugar cookies to him tomorrow with Maya. He loved that little girl—even if she did regularly beat him at Skip-Bo and Mexican Train.

I had just put the next round of cookies in the oven when I heard gravel crunch in the driveway. I did a giddy little dance as I took off my apron and went out to the front yard to see my girl. "Maya!" I cried happily.

"Livvy!" She dropped her duffel on the ground, running to give me a hug.

I picked her up in my arms, swinging her around. "I'm so happy you're home!"

Once I set her down, she said, "Daddy says you have a surprise for me?"

I smiled, nodded. "But you have to close your eyes."

Dutifully, she squeezed her eyes shut. Fletcher followed behind us, carrying her things as I guided her into the house. Then I said, "Open!"

She stared around the house, checking out all the decorations and the fresh cookies on the counter. "Can I have one?" she asked, going to the counter first.

Her dad and I chuckled, and he gave me a look like *Of course she would go for the cookies first.*

Smiling, I said, "Go ahead. I thought we could decorate the tree while we eat cookies and watch a Christmas movie?"

"Ooh! Can we watch *Elf?*" she said. "I love that one."

"Doesn't everyone?" I said with a smile. "Let's do it!"

Fletcher added, "I'll go put your bags up and come back to help."

While he walked away, I squeezed Maya again. "How long were you gone?" I asked her. "Like a year, right?"

She giggled. "Just a weekend."

"Oh, right." I smiled at her and brought her with me to the box of ornaments Fletcher had saved for them. I sat near the box, handing each of them to her while she explained what they were. Some, she'd had since she was a baby. Others, she picked out with her grandpa at the store or made with her mom.

I loved seeing all her memories, the way she smiled as she talked about them, how carefully she placed the really important ones on the tree. She was letting me into her world, trusting me with the precious pieces of her life.

"Do you have any ornaments?" she asked me.

"Actually…" I pulled a shoebox from under the coffee table. "These are mine."

I'd been collecting the flat, golden ornaments for as long as I could remember. The first one was a baby in a cradle and said "Olivia's First Christmas" with my birth year underneath.

I showed it to Maya and her mouth dropped open. "I didn't even know that was a real year."

"Maya!" I laughed, shocked.

Fletcher came to sit beside me on the couch. "Wait until she hears how old I am."

"I know you're about a million years old, Dad," Maya said with a roll of her eyes. Then she carefully hung my baby ornament right next to hers.

My heart swelled so much that the love over-flowed as tears.

I hurried to wipe them away so she wouldn't get overwhelmed by my emotion. But Fletcher caught me anyway. He tucked me to his side and whispered, "Is it everything you dreamed of?" Then he placed a kiss on my temple.

Maya pulled another ornament from my shoe-box, looking it over, and I had to smile as I replied, "It's not what I dreamed of… It's better."

RHETT AND MAGGIE'S BIG DECISION

1

———

MAGGIE

I MAY or may not have been staring at Rhett in his Wranglers as he hung up pieces of wire art around my new salon in Austin. My business in Cottonwood Falls had exploded. People loved the concept of Home, the experience of coming to the salon and feeling cozy and knowing they could hang out with a girlfriend while they got their hair done or bring their kids along without any shame or judgment.

So eventually it made sense to open up a new location. There were now three "Homes" in the towns surrounding Cottonwood Falls. And now? It was time to make a dream I thought was out of my reach come true.

Rhett and I wouldn't be living in Austin; instead, one of my best friends from cosmetology school would be managing the new location. I'd come to check in regularly, especially over the first year. Right now we were decorating for the launch happening the week after New Year's.

It was hard to believe it had been seven years since I uprooted my life in Austin and moved to Cottonwood Falls. Seven years since I reconnected with my high school sweetheart and realized what I thought was over was only just beginning.

Now? I couldn't be happier. Sure, we were busy with Rhett running his ranch and me running the salon, but getting to chase my dreams with my best friend was so worth it.

Rhett's voice brought me out of my trance as I heard him say, "Take a picture, it'll last longer."

My cheeks flushed slightly as I realized I'd been staring at his ass this whole time. I lifted my chin and said, "You know you look good."

He chuckled, climbing down from the step stool and wrapping his arms around my waist. All it took was the press of his lips to mine for me to forget the world around us for a moment. But when he pulled back, he said, "It's shaping up."

I looked away from his pretty hazel eyes, taking in the salon. The decor was simple, trendy, and warm at the same time. His wire art hanging on the walls was the perfect touch.

"It's really starting to come together," I said.

He grinned, looking around with me then he jumped slightly. "I have a brilliant idea."

I raised my eyebrows, having been witness to plenty of his brilliant ideas. Like the time he and Fletcher were in an escalating prank war for a solid year. Our tree still had remnants of silly string.

But he said, "You could hire full time cowboys for eye candy. I bet the ladies would *love* that."

I rolled my eyes at him. "Looking for a job?"

He smirked. "Are you saying I'm eye candy?"

My laugh came naturally. "You're great at fishing, didn't know that applied to compliments too?"

His laughter warmed me from the inside out. "Just gotta have the right bait." He gestured at his backside.

Giggling, I said, "Do you want to get some dinner, eye candy?"

"That sounds great."

We locked up the salon so it would be ready for my manager next week and then got into the truck and drove away. I navigated us to one of my favorite barbecue places in the city—one that I missed a ton living in Cottonwood Falls.

Together, we ordered more than enough food. But even though a feast like this usually pleased him, I could see there was something in his eyes, something he was thinking about and turning over his mind. "What is it?" I asked as I used a wet wipe to clean my fingers.

He looked up at me from his sandwich. "I just keep thinking about what's next."

"Next?" I asked. "I mean, depending on how this launch goes, we can try other metros in Texas."

He smiled, shaking his head slightly. "That's great, but I meant what's next for us."

I raised my eyebrows. "What do you mean?" I asked. We'd built our home to be perfect for us—there would be no moving away. And he loved owning his own herd of cattle.

"I know I'm aging like a fine wine," he said, "but I'm not exactly a spring chicken anymore."

I tilted my head to the side, waiting for him to explain.

"Children, Mags."

2

RHETT

I STUDIED HER FACE CAREFULLY, waiting for her reaction.

Over the years, we had visited and revisited the subject of starting a family, but the timing always felt off. First there was her opening her salon, and then there was me purchasing my own cattle herd and taking care of the animals. And then it was her opening another location and another location. And then it was me bringing on help, because I couldn't manage it all myself. But I was starting to wonder if there ever would be a good time for us. Or if a family just wasn't in the cards.

She looked down at the table and then pushed her plate away a little bit so she could fold her hands in front of her. "I guess I am getting older," she said.

I dipped my head in acknowledgement. Never in a million years did I think I'd be the kind of person to have to have this conversation, but time changed things. Now, there really was no getting around it. Even if she was sitting quietly, tossing thoughts around that pretty mind of hers. "What are you thinking?" I finally asked.

She shook her head slightly. "I thought I would know when I was ready for kids. But I haven't ever felt this burning need yet, if that makes sense."

I nodded, knowing what she meant. For a long time, Maggie and I felt like enough, but then my mom mentioned something about wondering if she'd ever see a grand-baby from me.

I told her not to rush me, but she pointed out that Mags and I may be running out of time, and it really got me thinking.

Seeing my sister and my brothers have children, I knew I'd miss having a family of my own. But I'd never want to do anything to make Maggie uncomfortable or derail her dreams.

Maggie looked up at me again. "I love my business," she said.

I nodded. "I know. You're changing lives, making a lot of women feel beautiful. Not to mention giving so many people jobs."

Her eyes shined at the compliment. "Thank you."

She picked up her fork and moved around some pulled pork that didn't look all that appetizing anymore. And then she sat her fork down again and said, "Can I have some time to think about it?"

"Of course," I replied. "I just feel like we need to decide, or the clock will decide for us."

She nodded slowly. "I understand."

We finished our dinner and then went to the hotel where we'd be staying before going back home the next day. At this point, we were so ingrained in our nighttime routines that the next hour felt like a well-oiled machine. She had all sorts of stuff that she put on her face before bed, and she'd even gotten me started on a skincare routine. I wasn't even mad about it—my face felt baby smooth, and I secretly liked the pampering at the end of a long day.

With her patches underneath her eyes and her hair up in heatless curlers, we slid into bed next to each other. I put out my arm so that she could lay her head on my shoulder, and we were silent for a moment, just breathing.

My hands splayed on her stomach. Her curves melded to my fingers, comfortable and familiar. Safe.

I knew if it was just the two of us, I would be okay. But there was still a part of me hoping that she would come around one day.

WHILE I DROVE BACK toward Cottonwood Falls, Maggie worked in the passenger seat responding to emails and placing orders for supplies. With my wife occupied, I listened to music and chatted on the phone with a couple of my family members. Gage was still living in Dallas, so we didn't get to see each other as often as I did the others.

I even got a call in to Cooper. He and Camryn were taking The Windmill Wagon and going out of town for Christmas with their kids. It was fun to chat with him, even if he had to yell at his kids every now and then, saying things like, *Do not touch your mama's bra!* and *Get the lipstick away from the dog!*

"I swear," he muttered, "It's like they wait until I'm on the phone to need me."

I chuckled, trying to ignore that little bit of jealousy growing in my stomach. I was happy for him and Camryn—especially since seven years ago I was doubting their quick marriage and family. But clearly, when you know, you know.

We pulled up to home and I smiled at the sight of our house illuminated by Christmas lights. They twinkled like the stars themselves had come down from the sky to celebrate the holidays with us.

All we had to do was get inside, unpack, and get ready. Tomorrow was Christmas Eve.

3

MAGGIE

THE NEXT MORNING, I went over to my mom's to make Christmas cookies. We had been back in each other's lives for a while now, but there was still so much time to make up for.

And going to my mom's place in town had me thinking even harder about having children. I had to be honest with myself and admit that my mom was a big part of the reason why I hadn't moved forward with having a family of my own. She had abandoned me when I was sixteen, and somewhere deep down, I worried that I had the gene that would allow me to do that to my own child.

Of course that's not something you can say to your un-estranged mother. *Hi Mom, glad you're back, but you also fucked me up for life and questioned my faith in motherhood* didn't really have a nice ring to it.

So I didn't say anything at all, focusing instead of mixing the cookie dough, getting the frosting exactly the right color.

My mom studied me across the table, stirring a bowl of red frosting. "You're quiet today."

I let out a sigh, still looking at the green frosting in my bowl. "Just in my head, I guess."

"What's going on?"

"I don't want to say," I finally answered. My chest already felt tight. Maybe part of me was afraid she'd leave again if I made her feel too bad for her mistakes, even though I knew it wasn't logical. She'd been around for years, had tried so hard to make up for lost time.

"Magnolia, you're scaring me," she said.

I looked up at her concerned eyes—a perfect mirror of my own—and said, "Is it okay if we have a hard conversation?"

I could see her shoulders tense a little like she was bracing herself, but she nodded. "What's going on?"

I chewed on my bottom lip. There really was no way to say this… "How could you leave me when I was just a kid?" I asked. She'd explained it to me before, but my brain still couldn't make sense of it, even as a grown woman.

I saw her eyes flutter closed. Her perfectly painted nails drummed on the table for a moment like she was trying to ground herself.

Seeing her uncomfortable wasn't great… She was my mom, but she was also the woman who left me for years, the woman I thought I would never see again. And her behavior had me seriously doubting motherhood myself.

"Sometimes when you're drowning, it's hard to think about getting your head above the water, much less think about anyone else," she said.

But my jaw clenched together. "Aren't parents supposed to think about their children first?" The words came out sharper than I intended, but I meant them.

She tilted her head, her eyes full of so much compassion for me, for herself. "I know what I did was wrong, but I didn't think you were drowning with me, Maggie."

My lips parted, her words sinking into my brain. All this time, I'd thought about what my mom had done. How she'd abandoned me, left her child all alone. I wondered if it meant I wasn't good enough, or if I didn't deserve her love somehow.

But what she was saying was the opposite.

She saw me as strong. Capable. Resilient. And

that's why she felt safe to focus on getting herself out of the abyss.

Maybe I needed to see myself that way too. I needed to see myself as someone capable of rising to whatever challenges I faced, who had a partner that would help me along the way.

"What brought this on?" Mom asked, breaking me from my thoughts.

My throat felt thick as I swallowed. "We're thinking about starting a family."

Her lips grew into a small smile. "I know I'm lucky to call you my daughter, but I think any kids you have would be luckier to call you Mom."

My eyes stung with emotion. I blinked them quickly, trying not to cry. "Thanks, Mom."

She patted my hand on the table. "Now let's focus on these cookies or Rhett will never let me hear the end of it."

4

———

RHETT

I CAME DOWN the stairs in our home, freshly showered and dressed for Christmas dinner with my family. I'd already gone and checked on the cattle, making sure that they had food and water available to them, checking to see if there were any sick ones.

The house smelled better and better the closer I got to the kitchen. Mags must have made the spice cake I loved to go with the sugar cookies she made with her mom.

When I rounded the corner into the kitchen, I saw her at the counter in her red sweater dress and boots. *Damn.* She looked incredible.

I leaned against the door frame, taking her in, wondering if I had it in me to go to Christmas dinner or if we should just head back to the bedroom.

She looked over at me watching her. "Sorry, my foil keeps ripping." She tore off another sheet of foil.

I folded my arms across my chest and raked my eyes over her curves. "I'm just admiring the view."

She rolled her eyes at me and teased, "Take a picture. It will last longer."

I pulled my phone out of my pocket. It made a loud shutter sound as I did just that.

"I was joking!" she said.

But I only smiled back at her. "I wasn't. You're so beautiful, babe."

"Thank you." She finally got the foil tightly around the edges of the pan, then smiled over at me. "I got you something for Christmas."

My eyebrows drew together. "It's Christmas Eve."

"And I'm impatient."

I chuckled and stepped forward to hug her, my boots heavy over our stone floor. "Is it you? Because I'd love to unwrap this dress."

She playfully hit my shoulder. "You're insatiable. Let me get it real quick."

My hands felt empty without her to hold, but soon she returned with a small box wrapped in gold wrapping paper.

When she handed it to me, I said, "I'm excited to see what you got me."

She seemed a little nervous as she said, "Go ahead and open it."

Finding an edge of paper, I peeled it back to find a white and pink box shrink-wrapped in plastic. Once all the wrapping paper was discarded, I had to read the box's label to make sense of it.

Ovulation detector.

I looked up at Maggie, chest already thrumming with hope at what this meant. Before I could say anything, she moved forward, taking the box from me and setting it on the counter. Then she held both of my hands like she needed me to steady her. If this was real, I needed her to steady me too.

"Rhett Griffin," she began, "I know that you're going to be an amazing dad one day. I love you, and I want to do this with you. Everything in life with you."

My eyes were already burning with emotion, so I pulled her close and kissed her until my breath was coming fast, and so was hers.

She giggled against my lips and said, "I didn't mean we had to start right now."

But I picked her up and lifted her onto the counter and said, "Why the hell not?"

KNOX AND LARKIN AND THE PICTURE FRAME

LARKIN

KNOX CAME into my house looking annoyingly good in a deep red sweater, jeans, and brown leather boots. If I wasn't holding three different bobby pins in my mouth, I would have bit my lip to keep from drooling.

But as it was, Emily was sitting in front of me, watching a movie on the TV while Jackson toddled around and played a game with his stuffed animals that I couldn't quite understand.

I mumbled a "Hey there" over the pins and he walked over to me, reaching for the pins. I let them out into his palm, trying not to be embarrassed about the drool. "Thank you," I said.

"Of course." He set the pins on the coffee table in front of me. "Can I help?"

Just then, Jackson realized Knox had come in and yelled, "NOTS!"

Knox grinned and picked him up. "Hey big guy!"

I smiled at the two of them. They had a special bond that made my heart all warm and fuzzy. "Would you mind putting Jackson's outfit on?" I asked Knox.

"Sure thing," he replied.

Jackson repeated, "Nots, nots," as he carried him back to his bedroom. He'd come so far in his speaking just in the last several months.

I finished working on Emily's hair, and when I finished the waterfall braids around her crown, I said, "Hold still. Let me spray it."

"Uh huh," she said, completely oblivious to anything but her show.

The couch springs squeaked as I got up and went to the bathroom for a bottle of hair spray. But on my way back, I stopped at Emily and Jackson's room. Knox had Jackson's sweater pulled over his head, but his elbows were bent in the sleeves. Knox was flapping Jackson's arm, saying, "Bawk bawk bawk, bawk," making Jackson laugh raucously.

There was nothing better than a toddler's full-body laughs. Especially since Jackson had been so withdrawn after the divorce. I'd seen my baby boy come out of his shell, start talking, walking, smiling more than he ever had before. And I knew it was because of all the joy Knox brought into our life.

Still smiling to myself, I turned away and went back to Emily. I covered her forehead with my hand and sprayed a good spritz on there so that her hair would stay in place throughout the photo shoot. This would be our first family photo shoot together, and would double as our engagement photo shoot. I wanted it to be perfect.

"Okay Em, I need you to go put on your sandals," I told her.

"Do I have to?" she whined.

"I could turn off the TV if it's distracting you?" I offered.

She quickly got up, going to the shoe rack by the front door, making me laugh quietly to myself. Nothing would come between that girl and Bluey.

But as she was walking back, she frowned at me. "Where are your shoes, Mama?"

I looked down at myself, still in my scrubs from work, and frowned. Of course I'd left myself to be the last one getting ready.

I hustled by the room where Knox was finishing getting Jackson dressed and went into my bedroom. Shucking my scrubs, I reached from the pretty velvet dress laid out on my bed. The cream colored fabric was soft under my fingertips.

Within minutes, I pulled it over my head and cinched the wrap around my waist, giving myself the appearance of an hourglass figure. I still hadn't lost this baby weight and doubt that I ever would. But with Knox, I was starting to accept myself, love myself, see myself through his eyes. That was one of the greatest blessings he could have given me other than loving my kids with his whole heart.

Now that I had the dress on, I slipped into a pair of brown leather booties and walked out of the bedroom. At least I'd curled and styled my hair this morning in preparation. Just a mist of hair spray and adjusting with my fingers had my look complete.

All three of them were in the living room, and all their eyes were on me as I walked in. I could feel their eyes on me, but Emily was the first to speak. "Mommy, you look like a princess," she gasped.

Those words had me all warm and fuzzy inside. "Thank you, baby."

Knox got up, holding Jackson in one arm. With his free hand, he gripped my fingers and spun me a circle. "Definitely a princess."

I grinned at him, loving the way he saw me. "You look very handsome, too."

"Are you ready to go?" he asked.

I nodded.

Together, we traipsed out to the truck to seal our perfect little family in photos forever.

2

———

KNOX

I LOVED HOLDING Larkin's hand as I drove down the road. Something about it just felt like home—especially with the kids chattering in the back seat. It reminded me that I was living out everything I ever wanted, thanks to this woman beside me.

We were going to take pictures on Madigan Ranch, and I couldn't wait. Even though it was wintertime, the countryside was still so gorgeous, with expansive grassland and panoramic views of the place where I grew up.

The drive there was as familiar as my own heartbeat, and a dozen minutes later, we pulled up to the meeting spot near the Madigan Ranch sign. A white Tahoe already waited there, pale gray exhaust spilling from the tailpipe while the photographer sat in the driver's seat, watching us approach.

She was the same person who had taken photographs of goat yoga on what I called our first real romantic date. She smiled at us as we got out of the car and held up her camera. "You guys ready?"

"Yes!" Emily said while Jackson screeched. Apparently he was not in the mood anymore.

Larkin cringed, shoulders deflating, but I said, "Don't worry, buddy." I picked him up and added, "We're going to have fun together."

The photographer had us all posed in no time, sitting in the grass, standing on the grass, holding the kids between us. All the while making silly faces and sounds to make Em and Jackson laugh.

There had to be a million different poses that felt awkward and unnatural, but whenever she showed us little previews on the camera screen, my chest swelled. The photos were perfect.

After we'd gotten plenty of pictures with the kids, Larkin settled them into the truck with candy and a tablet so we could take the engagement pictures. With the windows rolled down, they could yell at us if they needed anything.

Then we started posing just as a couple. The photographer said, "Hold her close and whisper your favorite ice cream in her ear like it's a dirty word."

I chuckled, not needing an excuse to pull my fiancé close. I made my voice low and sultry as I said, "Any type of ice cream with those brownies you make. I'll lick it off your naked body tonight."

Larkin giggled as her cheeks flooded with color and I heard the shutter of the camera go off at least a dozen times.

Then the photographer told us to walk back ten yards or so and then move towards her like we were coming home tipsy from a night at the bar.

Being our age, Larkin and I hadn't done that before, but for how much we laughed acting it out, I thought I needed to take her out and get a few tequilas in her.

My guy friends all complained about taking pictures with their girls, but the time seemed to fly by with Larkin. I could see how happy it made her to feel like a princess, like someone wanted to capture her image and admire her. And when we were done, I paid the photographer a little bit extra for the idea I was hoping I could make come true.

3

LARKIN

"MOMMY, do you think Knox will like the whoopee cushion I got him?"

I dumped a box of pasta into the pot boiling in front of me. "I think he'll love it. Just like he loves the other five he already owns."

The kids' ongoing prank war with Knox had continued in our dating phase and now our engagement. Over time, the pranks got more and more creative, but every so often, they went back to the classics. I wouldn't trade the joy it brought for anything. Even though sometimes I stepped on a mush banana or accidentally sat down on a toilet seat wrapped in cellophane, life was good.

Knox had hardly stayed the night at his place, opting to spend as much time as possible with us. Part of me felt guilty because I knew how much effort he'd put into purchasing his house and making it a home.

Emily said, "MOM!"

I realized I'd been lost in my own thoughts. "Sorry, hon, can you say it again?"

"Should I put it under the tree in the box?" she asked me.

"Why don't you go ahead and wrap it, Em, while I make dinner. You can draw on construction paper for the wrapping paper." She instantly got to work, grabbing a box of crayons and pink paper from the craft cabinet.

Jackson was playing with a roll of toilet paper, which might have upset me if he wasn't having so much fun rolling and unrolling it.

I ran a wooden spoon through the pasta to make sure it wouldn't stick and checked the clock. Knox was still working the night shift and should be here soon. I looked forward to the new year when he'd start working days.

"Done!" Emily called.

"Let me see," I said. She came over from the table and showed me an oddly shaped ball covered in construction paper and so much tape. I could see the outlines of two stick people on the paper with a heart between them. I smiled big and said, "Is that you and

Knox?"

She nodded.

"And how much tape did you use?" I asked, laughing softly.

"All of it." She grinned evilly. "It's going to be so hard to open."

I chuckled. "Of course, it's another prank."

She nodded and went to sit on the floor across from Jackson. Now they were rolling the toilet paper back and forth between them.

I smiled to myself, so thankful for them and their relationship with each other.

While they played, I took the chicken out of the oven, added sauce to the pasta, and heated green beans in the microwave.

With dinner done, I started plating it just in time for the front door to open and Knox to come inside.

I looked over my shoulder, seeing him freshly showered in a white T-shirt and a pair of sweats. I loved that he showered and was fresh for us after work. Just a little way to show he cared.

"Hey honey," I called over the kids greeting him.

He smiled, and then I realized he was holding something wrapped in red and white paper in his hands. He held it carefully to his chest as the kids ran up to him and grabbed each of his legs.

"Oh no, Larkin," he said, taking on a serious

expression. "My legs suddenly got *very* heavy. Do you know why?"

I carefully inspected him, pretending I was just as confused while the kids giggled maniacally. "I have no idea!" I finally said. "Your legs *do* look a little lumpy..." Emily and Jackson giggled. "Let me see if I can massage it out." I bent over, tickling them under the arms, and they both fell off his legs, laughing.

"Hey!" Knox said. "What are y'all doing down there?"

Emily popped up and said, "Is that present for me?"

He shook his head. "It's for your mama."

I smiled and asked, "Can I open it now?"

He nodded. "Let's go sit down."

We went to the living room, all of us sitting together on the couch while I tentatively pulled back the wrapping paper. Thankfully this one wasn't tape-mageddon.

Inside the wrapping was a picture frame with a perfectly framed photo, and I stared at it with my mouth open. "How did you get this? We just took them yesterday."

Knox nodded, "I asked her to do me a little favor."

I carefully ran my fingertip over the glass like I had to make sure the picture was real. It was just too perfect. The four of us looked like we *belonged* together. Knox was holding me to his chest while the kids romped around us in the golden grass. We were all smiling, surrounded by the countryside. My eyes started watering, and I had to sniff back tears before I broke down.

"What's wrong, Mommy?" Emily asked.

I shook my head, wiping at my eyes. "These are happy tears." I looked at Knox. "Thank you *so* much. I'll put this on the wall over the TV." I pointed at a blank spot right on the living room wall.

"Actually…" He paused. "I thought, maybe it could go somewhere else."

I looked around my home, wondering where he meant. "You think it would be better above the dining table?"

He grinned, shaking his head, "What if I found a plot of land for sale outside of town." He took my hand, lacing our fingers together. "And what if it has the prettiest oak tree that would make a great tire swing for Em and Jackson? And what if there's plenty of room for a big yard, a garden, and it's just a ten-minute drive into town, so you'd be close to your work and I'd be close to mine?"

Now the tears were threatening to fall again. "What are you saying, Knox Madigan?"

"I'm saying I thought we could build a home for

us, for our family, and I thought this picture could go right on the mantle when we do."

Holding back tears was futile, especially with how they were streaming down my cheeks. "You want to build a home with me?" I asked.

"Of course."

Emily said, "Can I see it?"

Knox said, "If it's okay with your mom."

I nodded excitedly. "I just made dinner, but we can put it in the fridge for now. I don't think I could eat anyway."

We put our plates in the fridge and all loaded up into his pickup. I held the photo on my lap as he took us out of town on a road that wound past Griffin Farms and Madigan Ranch. And then he took us down a gravel trail, and I spotted the oak tree with the sun setting behind it. There was a "for sale" sign nailed to a fence post.

My heart was already beating quickly as I took it in.

"Is this it?" Emily asked.

"It is," Knox said with a smile.

"Can we get out and look?" I asked.

"I thought you'd never ask."

I held the photo under my arm as we got out. It was an unseasonably warm night, like Mother

Nature knew we were too excited and forgot our jackets at home.

Emily immediately sprinted toward the oak tree over crunching brown prairie grass. Her hair swayed behind her as she ran, the sun glinting off her locks, and I could picture it. I could picture our home here.

Like a movie playing in front of me, I could see us watching the sunrise in the mornings, getting a picture-perfect sunset behind the oak tree every night.

Grass crunched underfoot as Knox came up beside me, letting Jackson down. He toddled after his sister, and tears streamed down my cheeks as I watched them.

"What do you think?" Knox asked.

I held up the photo, imagining it on a mantle place here.

Then I looked over at Knox and said, "I think it feels like home."

FORD AND MIA AND THE CHRISTMAS PARTY

1

———

MIA

"CAN YOU ZIP ME?" I asked Ford while I put on my green Christmas dress. I loved the way the color contrasted my pale skin and brought out the hint of green in my blue eyes. The piece had long sleeves and fell just above my knees, which looked perfect with my thigh-high black suede boots.

"Of course," he said. He came up behind me, first laying a kiss on my bare shoulder and then kissing down my spine. I was already starting to blush before he drew back and raised the zipper.

"Good?" he asked, his voice was hoarse, the action must have affected him the same way it did me.

I turned around, seeing him in his matching

green shirt and black slacks. He looked so damn good, and suddenly, I was very thankful that the Diamonds were not playing a game until two days after Christmas this year. Especially since it was our first Christmas together as a couple.

I turned to face him and linked my fingers behind his neck. He then lifted me onto the bathroom counter. "Have I mentioned how much I like these boots?" He ran his hand over the suede and even the adjacent contact had my skin flaming underneath.

"You do?" My voice came out breathy.

"So much." He hitched up my dress, dusting his fingertips over my thighs where the boots stopped.

I shifted my hips on the counter, wanting him closer. "What else do you like?"

He bit his lip and parted my legs so he could stand between my knees and speak right near my ear. "I like that I know what you're hiding underneath this pretty dress."

"You noticed?" I lifted my chin, giving him access to my neck. He took the invitation, trailing kisses from my jaw to my collarbone before reaching up to the strap of my thong and snapping it.

"So fucking hot."

I ran my fingers through the hair at the back of his head. "What else did you notice?" I asked.

"How easily I can pull the dress aside." He

tugged at the fabric, freeing my breast and caught my puckered nipple in his mouth.

My back arched into him, thighs already clenching. "We should get ready for the party… Our guests will be here soon…" It was a half-hearted excuse that he ignored by sliding his hands under my dress and finding my sensitive spot. He teased me with this thumb before pulling the fabric aside and sliding a finger into me.

"You shouldn't be so wet if you wanted to be practical," he hummed against my chest.

His words had my head falling back. The last thing I wanted right now was to be practical–his deft fingertips, his lips, the scrape of stubble against my skin–made sure of it.

Suddenly, he removed his lips from my chest, leaving a cool spot behind. I looked down to see him unzipping his pants, freeing his hard cock.

Instinctively, I licked my lips.

"Wrap your legs around me," he ordered, his gaze dark.

I knew to obey.

"Spit on it," he demanded.

I followed his directions, spitting on his cock between us and then using my fingers to spread it around before he surged into me.

I cried out in pleasure as I stretched to his size.

And then he pumped into me, building a rhythm that had me gripping the counter, holding onto his shoulders, clinging to him with my legs until I was shaking, shuddering, begging for release.

I was on the edge when I heard the doorbell ring.

"Shit," I muttered.

But he gripped my chin in one of his hands. "Look at me. I'm not answering that door until you come."

My eyes widened in surprise. My lips even parted, and he took advantage, putting his thumb in my mouth. "Suck," he commanded.

And again I obeyed.

"Eyes on me."

I followed his every instruction, my legs shaking, pussy begging for release.

And just as the bell chimed again, my body gave in to the last of Ford's commands. "Come with me."

And I did, crying out with how good it felt.

He shuddered against me, huffing out my name.

And as the last of the waves faded, I looked at him, my cheeks flushed pink, his hair askew.

The doorbell rang again, and I laughed. He dropped his head to my shoulder, smiling. "Think there's someone here?"

I bit my lip. "Someone's here? I had no idea. I couldn't hear them over my hair dryer."

He kissed me again, making me melt into him. Responsible? What's that?

FORD

I LIFTED up my pants and then handed Mia a washcloth, saying, "I'll go let everyone in."

My heart rate was still fast as I walked to the front door, passing by over-the-top Christmas decorations.

There were lights along the ceiling, decorations hanging in the windows, and even a sixteen-foot tree in the corner of my living room surrounded with piles and piles of presents for everyone in my family.

When I opened the door Mia's parents were standing there, noses pink from the cold. Each of them gave me a hug that I'm sure would be a little less warm if they knew what I had just been doing with their daughter.

I welcomed them inside, saying, "There are hors

d'oeuvres on the island and drinks in the fridge. Please help yourselves while I let the others inside."

They thanked me and went to the island as I watched my dad come down the driveway with my brother Knox, his wife, and their two kids. They must have ridden together, and I chuckled at the thought of Dad sitting in the backseat between the two carseats. I'm sure he had the time of his life.

"Hey, y'all," I said in greeting. "Come on in."

One by one, my family came inside. Hayes and his girlfriend. Liv, Fletcher, and their children. Bryce, carrying a bag full of gifts.

I followed them inside, shutting the door against the winter chill.

Heels clacked over my stone floors, and I looked over to see Mia coming into the room. She looked perfect as always, cheeks kissed with pink, her dress flowing perfectly over her curves, her smile warm and welcoming as she said hello to everyone.

I paused for a moment, taking it in. As if she could feel me watching, she met my gaze across the room, giving me a small smile. That was one of my favorite things about being with her.

We often went to events where we had to work the room, and I loved catching her gaze when we were apart. She always gave me a smile like we were the only two in on a secret.

"Son," Dad said a little loudly, looking exasperated.

"Sorry, what's up?" I asked.

He shook his head at me. "Been trying to talk to you for a minute straight. Too busy with the heart-eyes to pay attention to your old man?"

I rolled my eyes at him. "Sorry, Dad. What's up?"

"I was asking if you wanted to get started with presents? The kids keep asking."

"Sure thing," I replied. I wouldn't let them know that I already unwrapped mine.

HAYES AND DELLA'S HOT COCOA BOMBSHELL

HAYES

IT HAD BEEN a little over two years since Della and I started dating, and all the pink on the walls was starting to rub off on me—clearly—because at that moment, she had us dressed in matching Christmas sweaters that were pink with a white, smiling snowman on the front. But only because she could find one in Chopper's size. And because I agreed.

Don't tell anyone this, but I kind of liked being clearly labeled as hers. I was the only one who got the title, after all.

We had worked all morning decorating the house even more for the hot cocoa bomb party we were having with our families that day. There were indoor string lights shaped like snowmen, an obnoxiously festive tablecloth on the main table, and an extra folding table in the living room. On the kitchen counters, there was a hot cocoa bomb station where Della had laid out dozens of the things with different designs and flavors. Although, she told me she couldn't find one with mint flavoring. I was half ready to start a competing hot cocoa bomb company because it was bullshit not to include the best flavor, but now wasn't the time to think of that.

My dad, my brothers, their wives, their kids, and Della's parents were all coming over in just about ten minutes. If the Hayes from two years ago could've seen this, he would've thought he'd gotten a lobotomy. Maybe that's just what happens when you get married. (Just kidding.) It was more like I grew more of a brain, thanks to Della. Was that even possible?

Anyway, we also had a giant insulated jug of heated milk—and several thermoses with milk alternatives—because some people, for whatever reason, thought 2% wasn't good enough.

Della was still wearing her Christmas apron because she wanted to make her special sourdough sugar cookies for the event. The things didn't look like the sugar cookies you'd find at the store, but they actually tasted pretty good.

I walked over to her and gave her a hug, wrapping my arms around her curvy waist and kissing her as I fiddled with the tie to her apron. "Time to take this off. So all our guests can see our matching sweaters and tease me endlessly."

She giggled. "Why didn't we put the apron on this way?" she mumbled against my lips. Her tongue slid against my own lips and damn, I wanted to cancel the party and take her to the bedroom right then.

"Guess I wasn't smart enough back then," I mumbled as I kissed along her neck.

She giggled, making her skin vibrate. "You weren't smart enough a whole two hours ago?"

"Hey, I like to think I'm a grower." I pulled back from her neck to rub the tip of my nose against hers.

She laughed as I pulled the apron over her head. "That you are." Then she carefully smoothed her curls, even though trying to tame her wild mane was an act of futility. I liked her hair that way—wild. Opposite of my girl, who was so risk-averse she was always telling me some stat about how I was probably going to die of my own stupidity.

"Are you ready for the party?" she asked me, then nervously cast a glance around our home.

"Yeah, you?"

She nodded. "I think so." She bit her bottom lip. It took all I had not to tug it free with my thumb before she added, "Do you think we have enough hot cocoa balls?"

"You ordered two for every person," I retorted. "One's enough to send someone into a diabetic attack."

She laughed. "You say that like it's a bad thing."

I smiled back at her. "Well, then I think we're ready."

As if someone could hear our conversation, the doorbell rang. Della did a little happy dance, escaping my arms to go answer it. Smiling to myself, I hooked the apron onto her apron rack near the stove—because yes, Della had one for every occasion—and followed her to the door.

She opened it, letting in a gust of cold December air, revealing her parents silhouetted by the gray sky. They were just as punctual as she was, arriving about five minutes early.

When they came inside, I held out my hand to shake her dad's, then gave her mom a hug and a kiss on the cheek. She rubbed my back and I flinched—just a little—because of the new tattoo. But I did my best to hide the reaction.

"Good to see you, Mama," I told her. She had insisted I call her that, and it felt good to finally have someone to call "Mom" again.

"It smells wonderful in here," she said, glancing

around while she tugged off her mittens. "You two did a great job decorating."

"It was all Della," I said, taking her and Della's father back to the kitchen to show them the cocoa bombs and the cookies Della made while Della stayed in the doorway.

Looked like my dad was coming up the sidewalk, holding Aggie's hand.

Within fifteen minutes, it was a complete madhouse—kids running back to the guest bedroom to watch TV and play video games in the room Della had designed just for them. Adults mingled about the kitchen and living room, standing in the free spaces and catching up even though we all lived in the same damn town and saw each other all the time.

Della had once confided in me that people used to question why she had such a big house as a single woman, but I knew it was just her being sensible— preparing for moments exactly like this.

When everyone had arrived and the Christmas music had officially wormed its way into my brain, Della clapped her hands to get everyone's attention and said, "Hey! Let's get started!"

2

DELLA

I WAS PRACTICALLY BURSTING with excitement as all the guests in the living room and kitchen gave me their attention.

I grinned widely and said, "Welcome to the first annual Madigan Hot Cocoa Party!"

There was a little cheer that rippled throughout the room, and even Hayes cracked a smile. Chopper let out a happy little yip from his perch in the corner of the living room—a dog bed shaped like a throne.

"So everyone—fill your glass with milk and choose your hot cocoa bomb! We've got whipped cream and anything else you could want to add, plus my special sourdough cookies. I promise they taste better than they look!"

A polite chuckle rolled through our group of

loved ones. Standing there, seeing the group, I couldn't help but get a little emotional.

I had been used to going to my parents' house and having Christmas with just the three of us every year. I loved them and always enjoyed the holidays because they both worked to make it special. But this? I couldn't even begin to explain how special it felt.

After dreaming of having my own family for so long, my life just felt so much more complete with Hayes in it. Especially since his family was part of the deal. I loved them all so much—especially my best friend, Liv.

Everyone lined up to grab their hot cocoa bombs, and I stood next to Liv. I realized it was the first time in a while that she wasn't pregnant, nursing, or even holding a busy toddler in her arms. Crazy how life changed, but our friendship's stayed strong through every stage.

"Merry Christmas," I whispered to her with a smile.

She gave me a hug and said, "Have I mentioned how cute your house is?" She glanced around. "I couldn't create this much charm if I tried. And trust me, I have."

I laughed. "I love your house though." She and Fletcher lived in this gorgeous farmhouse outside of town with their four daughters.

"Me too," she said, a happy gleam in her eye.

"I remember getting ready for prom with you that year you went with him," I said.

Liv's cheeks grew red. "I'm sure I was so cringy."

Laughing, I replied, "You were the coolest. At least you didn't have to figure out how to accessorize a headset."

"True." She laughed.

I shook my head. "You were so excited, and you said, 'This could be the night that changes everything for us.'"

"It had," Liv said. "I just didn't know it then."

I smiled at the thought. It was crazy how things worked out. Hayes had told me while we were dating that he'd noticed me before but stayed away out of respect for my friendship with Liv—and because he just wasn't ready for a relationship yet.

There was something to the "right person, right time" theory.

Fletcher walked over, handing Liv a paper mug with Christmas symbols drawn in Sharpie on the outside—something Hayes and I had done the last few evenings while watching the holiday season of *Bake Off*. The cardboard sleeve even had a cute Santa sticker on it.

Fletcher said, "I'll let you pick your ball."

"Bomb," Liv corrected with a giggle.

Fletcher rolled his eyes. "You'd think you'd outgrow giggling at body parts."

"You're the doctor, not me," she tossed back and stuck her tongue out.

I smiled at my friend and her husband, grateful she had found her person, and that they were still so happy together. They walked over to the display of cocoa balls, already getting lower, and I heard people drinking their cocoa, talking about the different flavors and how good it tasted.

A heavy arm rested around my shoulders, and I looked over to see my dad. With a smile, I leaned my head over and rested it on his shoulder.

"Thanks for coming."

He kissed the top of my head like he used to when I was a little girl. "Always, honey. I was looking around for projects to do while people are busy talking, but..."

I looked over at him. "But?"

A slow smile spread across his face. "I can't find any."

A happy chuckle bubbled past my lips. "Hayes is on top of it."

Dad gave a nod of approval. "Glad to see it."

It wasn't an overwhelming show of support or a confession of love for my spouse, but Dad was great at showing in little ways how he loved me—and Hayes.

He winked, then walked off to fill a mug with hot milk and a cocoa bomb. Then my husband—the love of my life—came to stand beside me, slipping an arm around my waist.

"Looks like it's a success."

I settled my hand over his hand that rested on my waist and squeezed. "Thank you for putting this together with me. I know it's not your idea of a good time."

At that, he took his hand away from my waist and turned me so I was facing him. He held my face in both his hands and looked me in the eye as he said, "Any time I'm with you is a good time. I mean it."

I melted a little more. It was a miracle I wasn't a living, breathing puddle at that point.

"I love you," I whispered.

"Love you too." He kissed me softly on the lips and then pulled back.

And even though I was nervous, and my heart was racing, I said, "I have a special hot cocoa bomb for you in the kitchen. Come with me."

He drew his eyebrows together. "Did you find a mint-flavored cocoa bomb?"

I smiled back at him, thinking of the first time I had forced him to try mint hot chocolate—and his incredible poker face pretending he didn't like it. "Something like that," I said.

We walked further into the kitchen, where I had stashed a special mug on top of the fridge with a white hot cocoa bomb inside, decorated with a little pink and blue flower on top.

"Fill it up and tell me what you think," I told him.

He nodded, taking it to the jug of heated milk and pouring some of the steaming liquid on top. He shimmied his shoulders a little, looking absolutely adorable—even in the pink sweater I had convinced him to wear.

Then he grabbed a spoon and started mixing as he walked back toward me.

His eyebrows drew together. "What the fuck is this color?"

The cocoa bomb had opened up, and there was a mix of blue and pink. He looked at me and said, "Did you poison mine? Am I that bad of a husband?"

I giggled, shaking my head. "Look at the marshmallows. Can you tell what colors they are?"

His lips pressed together as he eyed the cup. "They're… pink and blue." Then he looked at me, confused. "It's cotton candy flavored?"

Even though there was a hum of conversation all around us, and I could feel his brother Knox watching us, I nodded and quietly prompted, "What typically comes in pink and blue?"

Hayes's eyebrows pinched together. Then his mouth fell open and he shouted, "Holy shit—we're having a baby?!"

I nodded, echoing, "We're having a baby!"

And that was when the party really began.

AGGIE AND GRAY SAY "MERRY CRUISEMAS!"

1

———

AGGIE

GRAY MADIGAN LOOKED hot as hell in a Hawaiian shirt, which is not something I ever thought I would say, considering I've known him for over 20 years and never once seen him in one. But as we waited in a massive line to board a cruise ship on Christmas Eve, he held my hand, rocking the palm tree print.

How did we end up on a cruise ship on Christmas Eve? Well, that's another story altogether.

It was just a normal fall day. We were sitting at the breakfast table, drinking coffee and eating the breakfast he'd made for us, when out of the blue, he said, "How do you feel about going on a trip?"

Of course, I was instantly excited because the amount of traveling I'd done in my life was next to nothing. So I nodded and asked, "What did you have in mind?"

He passed his phone across the table, showing me a picture of a cruise ship. It was a sort of collage, and I could see pictures of water slides, massages, and even lounge chairs with an ocean view. My eyes immediately went wide with excitement.

"Yes! When can we go?"

He chuckled. "Well, that's the thing. There's sort of a catch."

"A catch? At this point, I'd cut off my right ring finger to be able to go."

He raised his eyebrows. "What about your thumb? I need to know how much this is worth to you."

I laughed. "Just tell me."

"Well, a travel agent I know got us a great deal— but we'd have to leave on Christmas Eve."

Yet another stunner from this man.

"You want to spend the holidays away from your family?" I asked. He and his boys were so close, just like my kids and me. But we hadn't gotten together for Christmas in years. Isa still lived in Dallas and stayed on campus over the holidays so she could be a support to students who had families out of town. Enzo was finally back in Cottonwood Falls now, but he was seeing someone new and would spend the holidays with her family this year. He'd already warned me.

But Gray said, "I've spent over sixty years of my life celebrating Christmas with my family—either with my parents or my wife and children—but I have never gotten a Christmas alone to celebrate you. That's what I want to do this year. I want a trip just for the two of us, one where we can go and be alone and enjoy ourselves. What do you say?"

I smiled at him in disbelief, but also happiness. It sounded amazing—time for him and me to be together without the distractions of work, the ranch, or family. "I'd love that," I answered honestly.

He reached across the table, squeezing my hand, rubbing his thumb over the back of my knuckles. That gesture settled me in a way very few things could.

"I'll call my travel agent and get it booked today," he promised.

And he followed through on that promise, because we were now shuffling through the line with all sorts of people. Even as a waitress in a busy diner, I'd never seen so many people in my life. Gray told me this boat could hold around 6,000—which was almost as many as the whole town of Cottonwood Falls. I imagined our entire city climbing onto a boat and smiled to myself. Now that would be a party.

For the amount of people, they moved us through quickly. Soon, we were stepping onto the main level, and the first thing I thought was "opulent." There was a multi-story-tall art display, people singing, and a glittering bar filled with all sorts of drinks. And that was just this main level. Imagine what the rest of the boat had in store.

Someone spoke over the speaker system, telling us to meet at our muster stations, which they explained was a place to prepare for emergencies. I squeezed Gray's hand, a little nervous at the thought of an emergency on a cruise ship. We'd all seen Titanic at this point, hadn't we?

But he didn't seem bothered.

He said, "Let's go to the muster station and then check out our room?"

I nodded excitedly.

2
______

GRAY

I USED the little key card on my lanyard to let us into the suite. The room was on a lower level, which made me a little nervous, but the travel agent promised we'd hardly notice. But when we got inside, I realized she was right. Even though the room was small, it had enough space for a queen-size bed, a small desk, a bathroom, and even some closet space.

The bed had two towels folded up like swans facing each other surrounded by a heart of rose petals

Aggie covered her mouth but still couldn't hide the smile in her eyes. "Oh my gosh, this is so cute," she said. "How did you do this?"

"I told them it was our honeymoon, because every day with you is." I grinned at her, drawing her closer and holding her. "I'm excited to have seven days with you in this room."

She bit her lip, looking up at me with a twinkle in her eye. "Well, this room and the rest of the boat, right?"

I chuckled. "Not if I have my way."

She laughed in return. "It would be a shame to miss Jamaica."

I tilted my head to the side in consideration. "I suppose we can leave the room for Jamaica."

She smiled up at me, then tugged me down to kiss me deeply. With the fervor of her kiss, we soon found our way onto the mattress. My cock stiffened at her weight on top of me. Even though we'd been married for almost a year, it felt just as special as the day we'd gotten married. I ran my hand down her side, kissing her deeply, loving the way her body felt pressed against mine.

"Time for your first Christmas present," I murmured against her lips.

She smiled against my kiss. "What would that be?"

In answer, I shifted us so I was on top, then lowered myself, lifting the hem of her flowy skirt and tugging her panties aside. She gasped slightly, even as she spread her legs for me to gain access. Her pussy waited for me, fucking perfect. I slid my tongue along her slit, loving the way her thick thighs shivered against my ears.

"God, I love the taste of you," I told her.

She reached down, running her fingers through my hair. "Taste as much as you want."

My lips twitched into a salacious grin for just a second until my mouth was on her again. Every moan that escaped her mouth, every twitch of her fingers in my hair, every buck of her hips, encouraged me more. Turned me on until my cock was hard and begging to be inside her.

But I wouldn't allow myself that privilege, not until she came on my tongue and I devoured every drop.

I teased her growing nub with my tongue and filled her with my fingers while she made wordless sounds. Then her words came out gasping. "Keep going," she breathed. "Keep going."

Eager to please, I continued the same motion as her body went rigid and then convulsed, flooding my tongue with the taste of *her*.

A sense of pride went through me as her body shuttered and she cried out her release.

With her pussy still sensitive, I raised up, unzipping my jeans and then plunging into her sensitive hole. She moaned out again. "God you make me feel good," she said, holding onto my forearms.

"There's nothing better than you," I told her, meaning every word as I buried myself inside her time and time again. "Nothing sweeter than you. Nothing."

Her eyes filled with moisture. "I love you, Gray."

My chest swelled, and I had a hard time holding back my orgasm. "I love you, Aggie." I stayed still for a moment, looking into her pretty brown eyes, relishing the warmth of her pussy around my cock. The softness of her belly against mine, the mash of my hips against the back of her thighs.

And as the urgency faded, I drove into her again. She reached down with her fingers, rubbing herself as I thrusted. The sight of her hand working near my cock was incredibly hot. Especially the way it made her tighten around me.

"That's it," I told her. "Make yourself feel good."

She nodded, moaning out, "Mhmm."

"So fucking good," I told her. "Just like that."

Her eyes squeezed shut, her walls tightening in ripples around my cock.

"Keep going," I told her this time. "You're going to come for me again."

"I am," she whined out. "I'm..." She gasped again, right before an urgent little moan. Feeling her come apart gave me the permission I needed to do the same.

I pulsed into her, crying out with the force of our orgasms meeting. *This is what it was supposed to feel like*, I thought as we shook together. This match of love and lust and trust and everything in-between.

When the waves faded, I lowered myself to the bed next to her and pulled my pants back up, feeling spent. I held her hand as we caught our breath, fingers intertwined. We were both fully dressed, but that hadn't gotten in the way one bit.

A knock sounded on the door, and we scrambled up in the bed like two teenagers. I got up, wiping my face on one of the towels in the bathroom on the way as Aggie stood and straightened her outfit.

At the door, I glanced back to make sure she was decent and caught sight of her smoothing out her hair.

I smiled at her, "Decent?"

"In body only. Not in spirit."

I chuckled. "Good enough." And then I tugged the door open.

At the door was one of the crew's employees, dressed in a blue uniform.

"Are you two enjoying your room?" he asked.

I glanced back at Aggie. "Are we?"

Aggie's cheeks flushed as said. "We sure are."

We'd barely been on the boat for an hour, and our vacation was off to an incredible start.

3

___

AGGIE

I AWOKE on Christmas morning having slept better than I had in my entire life. Something about the rocking of the boat and the pitch black room had lulled me right into a deep, dreamless sleep. When I woke, folded into Gray's arms, I wondered if I was on a cruise ship or in heaven. Maybe both.

I rolled over in his arms, kissing his lips.

"Merry Christmas," I murmured.

He let out a small sigh as he woke up. "Merry Christmas, baby." His voice was so sexy when it was all scratchy and tired.

I smiled at him in the darkness, feeling like this was the gift—just him and me, being together for a holiday. But then he murmured, "I think Santa paid us a visit."

I raised my eyebrows at him. "Are you calling morning wood a present?"

He barked out a surprised laugh. "No, silly. There's a present for you on the desk."

Snuggling into his chest, I asked, "How did Santa get in this room without a chimney?"

He chuckled. "Best not ask questions."

Feeling giddy to open a present, I got up and flipped the light switch.

"Aggie!" he moaned. "You're gonna blind me."

I laughed. "I had to see my presents, old man!" To be fair, my eyes were stinging too, but I wouldn't tell him that.

He sat up on the bed as both of our eyes adjusted. I laid my eyes on a stocking hung on the mirror with a hook attached to a suction cup, and below it was a square, wrapped box.

I stared back at him in amazement. He must have set this all up after I went to sleep. "Thank you. It's so pretty, I almost don't want to open it."

"Well then, I guess we can go back to bed then," he retorted, leaning over to switch the light back off.

"Hey, hey, hey!" I said, laughing. "*Almost* too pretty to open!"

"Ah, I see." He lowered his hands, still giving me a smile that could melt chocolate.

Still smiling myself, I pulled down the stocking

and started taking out the items. I remembered my mom giving me a stocking each Christmas up until I was about twelve or thirteen—close to when she married my stepdad. She never had money for much besides that, but it was fun to get an orange and a few little trinkets each year. I missed it when she stopped.

So getting a stocking from Gray, at my age, felt even more special. Inside was a candy cane-shaped container filled with candy, a pack of silk hair scrunchies, several different brands of lipstick I'd been wanting to try, and even a contouring palette I'd told Gray was just a little too expensive for me to purchase a month or two ago.

As I pulled out the items, it was hard to keep from crying with joy. The fact that Gray had listened to all the little things throughout the year and made them come true for me made me feel so loved. I just wished I could make him feel the same way.

"Gray, I'm sorry I didn't get a stocking for you."

He shook his head, smiling. "I unwrapped my present last night, remember?"

I shook my head at him, going to kiss him. "I thought that present was for me."

"I'm sure it was," he replied.

I smiled, going back to the little desk in the room to look at my other present. I opened the box, and inside there was a ring and a matching bracelet.

They were shining silver with diamonds attached and looked awfully expensive.

I stared at him in shock. "What is this?"

He said, "I know we've haven't been married all that long, but I've been in love with you for a long time, even when I was scared to admit it. And in a couple of weeks, it'll be the anniversary of the day we first met—the 25th anniversary, which is silver. So I know you were talking about cutting your right ring finger off to come on this cruise, but maybe you could put this ring on there instead—as a reminder of how much I love you."

Now the tears were really falling. It was early in the morning. I'm sure I looked a mess, with no makeup on and my hair still in its silken bonnet, now with tears in the mix—but I went to him and hugged him, his arms wrapping tight around me.

"You have no idea how special this is to me," I mumbled into his strong chest.

He kissed the top of my head. "I just want you to know how much I love you. Always, Aggie."

"I know," I told him as I pulled back to look at him. Since he'd committed to me, he'd never given me reason to doubt his feelings. "Now it's time for your present."

He leaned back, pretending to pull down his pajama pants.

I laughed, hitting his shoulder playfully. "Not that! There's time for that later."

He grinned salaciously. "Well, I'm looking forward to that present—and whatever the other present is."

Chuckling and shaking my head, I went to the small closet and got out my carry-on bag, pulling out the wrapped present I had gotten for him. I handed it to him and sat beside him on the bed amongst the wrinkled sheets. He peeled back the red wrapping paper and lifted the lid to the white cardboard box, revealing the special-order hatband I'd gotten for him to add to his cowboy hat.

It was a leather band, braided in five thin strands. On the side was a silk sunflower and a cosmo so they would last forever. There was also a feather his grandchildren had found for him one day while they were out on a walk by the house. He'd brought it home and set it in his dresser drawer, that's how special it was for him. I'd taken it and had it preserved for this hatband.

As I explained all the pieces to him, his eyes grew misty and his voice hoarse with emotion.

"Aggie, this is too much."

I shook my head. "You might be a cowboy, but you're a sentimental man, too. And I knew you'd want to carry reminders of those you love with you every day."

He drew me closer and kissed me passionately.

And even though the buffet upstairs was full of treats, we missed breakfast in lieu of something even sweeter.

4

GRAY

AS WE SAT at the breakfast table enjoying an early meal together, we could see the next port through the window. It was a gorgeous green island, and it captivated my gaze—so different from what I saw every day. Although it was hard to focus too much with Aggie staring at it gleefully.

"It looks kind of like Hawaii from the airplane," she commented, a bittersweet tinge to her voice.

That had been a hard time for us all, the time she'd spent in Hawaii to help nurse Enzo back to health. Thankfully, her son was in much better health now. In fact, you almost couldn't tell he'd ever been so injured—unless he wore shorts, then you could see the scars. He worked as a firefighter for Cottonwood Falls and did his duties well.

We finished eating our breakfast together—which my Fletcher would be glad to know included a helping of fruits and vegetables—and then went to our room to grab our things for the day. Aggie wanted to spend it at a beach outside of Nassau. It sounded like a grand plan to me, even though I hated the feeling of sand getting caught in my leg hair. She told me that wasn't a sexy thing to say out loud. I'd take her word on it.

Getting off the boat in the massive crowd wasn't particularly fun, especially considering the number of people I usually saw in a day was ten. But we made it out of the port and into the back of a taxi cab with a chatty driver who told us all about the island as he drove us to what he promised would be one of the more remote beaches in the area.

Neither Aggie nor I wanted to spend time at a tourist stop surrounded by people—we wanted something just for us to enjoy.

Eventually, he pulled the car around to what looked like a cliffside with a gap in the railing.

"It's down there," he said.

Aggie and I both stared at him, looking for a hint of a trick in his dark-brown eyes. "Are you sure?" she asked. "It looks like a death trap."

He chuckled heartily. "There's a set of stairs that will lead you down to the beach. It's a small beach—

just locals go here—and it won't be busy this time of the week."

I gave Aggie a look to ask if she thought this was okay, and once she nodded, I asked the driver, "You'll come pick us up in a couple hours, right?"

"When you hear me honking, I'm here," he confirmed.

Hopefully he was right—otherwise it would be a long walk into town. The thought of being stranded here made my chest feel tight, but I reminded myself that I was okay. Everything was okay as long as I had Aggie.

So the two of us got out of the car, and it zoomed away as we walked to the gap in the railing. I stared down the cliff—it was about twenty feet down. The concrete stairs were a little crumbly and the railing looked rusty, like this place had been forgotten long ago. But we walked and scooted our way down, taking it plenty slow just to be safe.

When we were finally at the bottom of the sandy basin backed by cliffside, I was in awe of how beautiful it was.

This was like something out of the movies, with deep sand, gentle waves, and clear blue sky as far as the eye could see. There was no one around—just the two of us.

"This place is perfect," I said.

Aggie agreed and lay our towels out in the sand. "I can't wait to feel the water." She must have meant it because she shimmied out of her shorts and took off for the water.

"Come join me!" she tossed over her shoulder, her words floating in the breeze.

And as I pulled off my T-shirt and chased after her, I thought, *This is the best Christmas ever.*

AFTERWORD

I hope you've enjoyed these fun, short, Christmas themed stories about each of the amazing couples from the Hello series. This compilation of stories featuring plus-size, curvy heroines and hot sexy heroes who love every curve is my love letter to you. It's time you know that you are loved and seen and deserve to be treated like these beautiful women in this book.

Though this is the end of the Hello series, it's not the end of steamy, heartfelt romances for all sizes.

Check out www.KelsieHoss.com and sign up to my email list to get all the special deals and discover which book is coming out next!

The Hello Series

Hello Single Dad

Hello Fake Boyfriend

Hello Temptation

Hello Billionaire

Hello Doctor

Hello Heartbreaker

Hello Tease

Hello Quarterback

Hello Trouble

Hello Handsome

JOIN THE PARTY

Want to talk books with Kelsie and other readers? Join Hoss's Hussies today!

Join here: https://www.facebook.com/groups/hossshussies

ABOUT THE AUTHOR

Kelsie writes steamy rom coms that will make you laugh, cry, and dream of happily ever after! Her heroines are real, curvy women and her heroes are the kinds of men we deserve!

In all of Kelsie's books, you'll find heartwarming moments and plenty of laughter.

She currently lives in Colorado where she

watches way too many rom coms, chases her three boys up the mountains (huffing and puffing), and writes books for lovely readers like you.

Connect with Kelsie (and even grab some special merch) at kelsiehoss.com.